CAUGHT UP

L.A. Fowlkes

All Scripture quotations are taken from the King James Version of the Bible.

Caught Up
ISBN 0-9723759-0-2

For Information:
FowlkesBooks
P.O. Box 862
Lithonia, GA 30058
www.fowlkesbooks.com

Interior format and typesitting by Rodney Fowlkes
Cover by FowlkesBooks, Lithonia, GA
Section Interior Art work by Shadrick Wright
Production coordinated by Rodney Fowlkes

Dedication

To my husband, Rodney L. Fowlkes, whom God in His infinite wisdom and matchless love has bonded us together to bring forth His perfect will and divine destiny.

To My Heavenly Father.
To Thine Be The Glory!

The Departure

Caught Up

Chapter 1

All around the trees were heavy with leaves. The ground beneath her feet was soft and covered with fallen leaves and wildflowers. She knew that she had come here before and yet it looked as if no one had ever come here before for there was no worn path. Her feet moved of their own as if they knew the way. They take her to a waterfall that is in the midst of a clearing in the dense foliage. The water falls softly and yet she cannot see it's beginning or end. Looking around she can see animals and even birds and yet something seemed amiss. She soon realized that what seemed unusual was that all around her there was life and yet there was no sound except that of the waterfall and it was so soft that even standing close to it she had to strain to hear it. She sat down on a large rock near the falling water, close enough that she could reach out and feel the water run over her extended hand. She cupped her hand *catching a small amount and drank of it. It was cool and inviting. It was unlike any water that she had ever tasted and as she drank her fill of it, a peace such as she had never known filled her and she lay beside the water upon the soft carpet of leaves amid the wildflowers. And she slept.*

The alarm clock jolted her from a deep sleep. Alyson extended a groping hand to silence the intruder. She fervently believed that alarm clocks were a menace to society and was about to push the snooze button when the phone rang blaringly. The ringer was on its loudest setting because she'd been known to sleep right through the ringing! When she picked up the receiver, all she could manage was a begrudging "Hello."

"Hey girl, are you up yet?"

"Of course I'm up," Alyson answered her sister Alicia sarcastically, grimacing into the phone.

"Liar," Alicia said, not at all disturbed by her sister's morning attitude. "How about lunch, one o'clock at the Magic Chef?"

"Sounds good," Alyson said grimacing again into the phone.

"I see you're in a good mood this morning. Now repeat what I just said about lunch."

"I know what you said." Alyson could here the laughter in her sister's voice.

"Then repeat it. I want to make sure you heard me."

Alyson reluctantly obeyed and repeated groggily, "Lunch, one o'clock at the Magic Chef."

"Good girl," Alicia said. "I'll see you then."

It was a full minute before Alyson realized that her sister had hung up. The computerized voice of the operator sounded blaringly in her ear... 'If you wish to make a call.' Alyson hung up the phone and lay staring unseeingly at the ceiling trying to come to full consciousness.

She and her sister were twins, born five minutes apart, first Alyson then Alicia. Though they were not identical twins the family resemblance was strong. Outwardly without a doubt any stranger could tell that they were sisters, but there the similarities ended for they were complete opposites in every other respect.

Alyson rubbed the sleep from her eyes. She was definitely not a morning person, but her sister Alicia was every bit one! Thank goodness her job as hospital administrator for Heritage Medical Center afforded her flexible hours, because her logical thought processes didn't even kick in until at least ten o'clock a.m.! Her sister on the other hand was up long before six a.m. every morning. Even though her position as Director of Nursing Services at The Women and Children's Hospital didn't require her to be at work until eight a.m., she was always promptly there by seven a.m.

They had both decided on a career associated with medicine, although for very different reasons. She wanted to have an impact on hospital reform from a business standpoint and her sister Alicia wanted to approach change directly from the patient's standpoint. Atlanta, Georgia afforded them a large enough population to really explore the depths and heights of their respective careers. It had been home to them all their lives.

Alyson was aggressive and outspoken, Alicia mild tempered and soft spoken and yet both were just as effective in getting the job done. The list of differences stretched from birth to thirty-one years strong and yet in spite of those dissimilar traits, attitudes, and outlooks, no two could have been closer. The bond they shared had strengthened over the years into a stronghold that both cherished and nurtured.

Alyson sighed heavily as she rolled out of bed and headed to the shower, "Another day, another dollar," she murmured to the silent apartment. She and her sister had been roommates throughout college, but had gotten separate apartments afterwards in order to give each other their respective space, never mind that they saw one another practically every day any way!

When Alyson arrived at her office there was already a stack of phone messages. She logged onto her computer and sat back in her chair savoring the cup of coffee she had grabbed on her way in. Undaunted by the many e-mails, she clicked on her task list and typed in a couple of additional things that needed immediate attention and checking her calendar for the day she made sure that she was free at one o'clock for lunch with her sister.

The morning was a blur of meetings, first one committee then another. Checking her watch, Alyson had just enough time to get to the Magic Chef. She wanted to surprise her sister and get there on time for once!

The restaurant was a block from the hospital complex and was a favorite among the staff. It was usually crowded at lunchtime, but since it was almost one o'clock, the bulk of the crowd had already eaten and left. Alyson didn't see her sister outside the entrance, so she went inside. She looked around after her eyes adjusted to the change in light, but didn't see Alicia seated among the patrons there. She proceeded to the outdoor terrace and took a seat at a vacant table where she could see the entrance and relax in the cool shade with a large glass of iced tea.

She had taken the liberty of ordering Alicia a glass also. The tea was cool and refreshing. She sipped slowly as her eyes absorbed her surroundings. It really was a beautiful day. Atlanta was breathtaking in the spring. The temperature hovered at 75 degrees with a slight breeze that carried with it the fragrance of fresh flowers in bloom.

Halfway through her tea she glanced at her watch. It was one thirty and still no Alicia. The ice was nearly melted in her sister's glass of tea and the outside of the glass was beaded with drops of condensation. This was not at all like Alicia. She was always prompt and even if she thought that she was going to be delayed, she would have called to let her know. Alicia checked her cell phone to make sure that she had not inadvertently missed a call. There were no calls in her voice mail. She checked her beeper to make sure she had not missed a call and she came up empty handed. Alyson resolved to give her sister a few more minutes before she called her. Perhaps there had been some crises at the hospital and she just hadn't had time to call.

A few more minutes turned into twenty more minutes and still no Alicia.

Alyson tried to call her sister's cell phone to no avail. She thought it odd that Alicia didn't pick up for she carried it everywhere and was meticulous at keeping it charged. She tried her beeper and waited for a response. At 2:00 p.m. her attempts to reach her sister were still unfruitful. At 2:15 p.m. Alyson gave up. Looking at her sister's untouched glass of tea, the ice long melted, and the condensation all but absorbed into the napkin underneath it, she wondered for the hundredth time what could have happened to her sister. It wasn't like Alicia to stand her up.

Alyson paid the waiter for the drinks and left the restaurant still puzzled. Returning to the hospital, she grabbed a sandwich at the hospital cafeteria and ate it at her desk. Repeated attempts to reach her sister failed with only her sister's voice mail picking up at her desk.

At 4:30 p.m., Alicia still had not phoned. Alyson decided to call the secretary of nursing services. Through their conversation she found out that Alicia had had to go to an emergency meeting at one of the hospital's satellite locations. The meeting was at ten o'clock that morning and they had expected Alicia back long before now. The concern in the secretary's voice did not go unnoticed by Alyson.

"Are you sure she didn't come in and you just didn't notice?" Alyson asked, grasping for any explanation.

"No, I just went into her office to put a stack of phone messages on her desk, and she always checks in on her return if she's been off-site. I've tried repeatedly to beep her and so far there has been no response."

"Yeah, so have I," Alyson said distractedly biting down on her lower lip. "If she returns before you leave today, please have her phone me."

After hanging up the phone, she still didn't have any answer as to her sister's whereabouts. She worked until 7:30 p.m. Since she had no husband, no children, and no pet except her goldfish Charlie, she often worked late into the evening. Deciding to call it a day, she turned off the lights in her office and resolved to stop by her sister's apartment on her way home.

Her knocks went unanswered so she opened the door with the key her sister had given her. They had swapped keys in case one of them ever got locked out or inadvertently lost their key. With the flick of a switch, light flooded the living room of the apartment, which was meticulously neat and tidy. It practically put her own to shame in comparison, though she was by no means a slob. She simply liked a place to look lived in. Another one of their differences!

It didn't look as if Alicia had been home since that morning. Alyson left a note and went home to her own apartment that was only minutes away. Her answering machine light was blinking. Alicia had probably phoned, but after checking the messages recorded, none were from her sister. Now she was worried! Should she call her parents to see if they had seen or heard from Alicia? No, she didn't want to worry them unnecessarily, for her mother would easily sense the worry in her voice. She'd give it just a little more time, after all Alicia was a grown woman and not some little child that hadn't come home from school.

Alyson often brought work home and after popping a frozen dinner into the microwave, she delved into her work to keep her mind occupied.

It was nine o'clock and still no word from Alicia. Alyson tried again to phone her apartment and still there was no answer save the one on the answering machine. "Alicia where are you?" Alyson questioned aloud.

She had no choice now but to phone her parents. She would be careful not to alarm them for she knew that her parents would immediately have the police, the search and rescue squad, and the whole neighborhood involved. She would just see if she could get any information in an indirect sort of way to calm her own growing fears.

"Hey Mom, how are things?"

"Fine dear," her mother's voice sounded as if she herself was concerned about something.

"How's Dad?"

"He's doing fine."

"Mom is everything okay?" Alyson sensed that everything was far from fine.

"Oh I'm sure it's nothing. I was just about to call you. I was wondering if Alicia was at your place. She was suppose to stop by and have dinner with us this evening but we've not heard from her."

"She was supposed to have dinner with you this evening?" Alyson repeated, her worry now escalating with each passing moment. "Mom I was hoping that you'd heard from her," Alyson said, her initial objective of being a discrete detective forgotten.

"It's so unlike her to make plans and simply not show?"

"I know Mom, but try not to worry." She dared not tell her about the planned lunch date that had not happened with Alicia. "I'll make a few phone calls. She's probably down at the food bank or something. You know she always has some charity project going."

"You're probably right."

Alyson called every place she could think of and all were fruitless. Now she began to worry in earnest!

The next morning Alyson awoke feeling tired. She had stayed up much of the night repeatedly calling Alicia's apartment and she'd had that dream again of walking through the forest and coming to the glade with the waterfall. Pushing the dream aside, Alyson got up and showered. The shower freshened her resolve to get some answers today! This was not at all like her sister to be out of touch with her family. A call to her sister's office was answered by the secretary and she was informed that her sister had not reported to work as was her usual by seven a.m.

It was almost eight a.m. when Alyson arrived at her sister's apartment. It looked just as it had the night before. Even her bed looked as if it had not been slept in. Her car was not in its customary place in the parking lot, nor was it anywhere that she could see in the entire parking lot.

Though Alyson knew she needed to call her parents, first she would contact the police. She started to call from her cell phone, but decided to go in person instead.

The Dekalb County police headquarters wasn't far from the hospital and after phoning her secretary, she made her way through the morning traffic. After being directed to three different places in three different buildings she hoped that she was in the right place this time. After going through the metal detectors, she stopped at the information desk to find out whom she could talk to about her predicament. She was directed to room 215 on the second floor where a tall thin man who introduced himself as Detective Michael Dennison answered her knock and directed her to a chair opposite a large desk.

"What seems to be the problem?" he asked as he took his seat behind the desk.

"It's my sister," Alyson began tentatively; "No one has seen or heard from her since yesterday morning and I'm concerned that something has happened to her."

"Before you can file a missing persons' report the person in question must be missing at least 48 hours," Detective Dennison said calmly.

Alyson had been avoiding the word missing, but there it was just the same and she could feel it as it settled itself on her shoulders and she feared that they would not be able to bear the weight of the implication of that one little word. She didn't realize that she had been sitting motionless until the detective asked her if she was okay.

"My sister would never be out of contact with her family or miss a day of work without calling in." Alyson said willing herself to stay in control of her thoughts.

"I'd like to ask you some questions and I'll need you to try and remember anything you can even the smallest detail," the detective said as he reached for a pen and a notepad. "I'll need her full name and marital status and your name as well since we will be filing the report on your directive."

Alyson proceeded to tell him what she could. She began with the conversation the previous morning and ended with her sister's still empty apartment.

"Are you sure she's not just with a boyfriend?"

"No she's not seeing anyone."

"Are you certain," the detective persisted.

"Yes, I'm certain." Alyson answered, the agitation in her voice apparent. "We are very close. If she was seeing someone she would have told me." Wouldn't she? The question came uninvited to her thoughts, but she quickly pushed it aside, agitated for thinking such a thing in the first place.

"What about drugs?"

"What about drugs?" Alyson repeated.

"Has your sister been known to use drugs?"

"No!" Alyson replied indignantly.

"I'm sorry Ms Edwards, but I have to ask these questions."

"I know you have to ask these questions, but you don't know Alicia. She is the epitome of the most perfect sister to me and daughter to her parents. She has the most admiral traits of anyone I've ever known. She is kind hearted and trustworthy, dependable and so thoughtful of others. I know without a doubt that something is not right. Please help me. I don't know what else to do." Alyson didn't try to conceal the pleading tone in her voice.

"At this point, all we can do is make a few calls; hospitals and shelters. We'll need a recent picture of her and a description of her car. We'll also need a number where you can be reached. We'll do what we can. If she hasn't materialized by tonight, we'll begin our investigation." He rose and Alyson followed his lead.

"Thank you for your help," Alyson said in earnest, relieved that she now had made some progress in her search. She gave him the picture she had of Alicia from her wallet.

"This is my card. Please contact me if you hear from her. I'll give you a call tonight and let you know if the area hospitals or shelters turn up anything."

Alyson sat in her car for a long time trying to calm down. Since leaving the police station and unusual feeling had spread through her. It was unsettling in that it was indescribable. She couldn't remember ever feeling this way before. She tried again in vain to put a name to it. It wasn't fear, or trepidation or even apprehension. "Alicia where are you," she said in a small voice not caring that to people passing by she appeared to be talking to herself.

She started the car and left the complex mass of buildings and pointed her car in the direction of her parent's home.

Chapter 2

Pulling into her parent's driveway she remembered how shocked she and her sister were when they had moved into this house a few years ago after her father had retired. It was nothing like the Victorian style house in which she and her sister had grown up in. Though the house was different the yard was just as spectacular. Her father was a genius at landscaping. The driveway was lined with flowering bushes in white and crimson and the stubby branches of the dogwood trees were laden with pink blooms. There were flowers in bloom everywhere one looked. Her father's handy work was a small mirror of why Alyson so loved Atlanta in the springtime of the year. There was such beauty that it almost took one's breath away. She usually stopped to admire it, but not today.

She used her key to let herself in the front door. The aroma of bread baking filled her senses making her mouth water and reminded her that it was almost noon and she had not eaten anything. Her mom use to bake bread all the time when they were growing up, but now she only did so on holidays or when she needed to 'gather' her thoughts, and since it wasn't a holiday....

"Mom, Dad, where are you?"

"In the spare room dear."

She could hear her mother's voice coming from a room down the hall. She found them both knee deep in parts. "What's going on?" Alyson asked as she hugged her mom then leaned over to kiss her dad on the forehead for he seemed unable to extricate himself from the debris.

"I'm putting together this piece of exercise equipment for your mom. You know she wants to keep that girlish figure!" Her father answered winking at Alyson and laughing softly.

"Mom, Dad, have you heard from Alicia?" Immediately she could feel the tension in the room.

"No, we were hoping you had. I can't imagine what could have gotten into her. She's never acted this way before."

"I called her office this morning and she didn't go in nor did she call in." Alyson let realization sink in before she plunged ahead. "I went by her apartment and nothing was different from the last evening. Her bed had not been slept in." Alyson finished quietly.

"What are you saying Alyson?" Her mother was holding her hand over her heart.

"I'm saying that no one has seen or heard from Alicia since just before noon on yesterday."

"What are you saying Alyson?" This time the question came from her father who had risen from the pile of parts.

"I'm saying that I've just come from the police station and they are filing a missing person's report at my request."

At that her mother collapsed onto the weight bench. "Alicia is missing? My child is missing?"

"Mom we don't know that." Alyson tried to comfort her mother. "Dad when was the last time either of you talked to or saw her?"

"She called about mid morning yesterday and said that she would be by to have dinner with us," he answered as he put the tools away and began pacing the floor.

"Did she sound okay?"

"As I recall, nothing seemed out of the ordinary," he replied, scratching his own head as he said it to hide his own growing fears.

"Honey, what did the police say?" her mother asked.

Alyson went over all the details of her earlier meeting with Detective Dennison.

She soon left her parent's house. Each promised to call if either heard from Alicia. Alyson went on to work with a heavy heart, after deciding against returning to Alicia's apartment to wait the day for her to show up. She had plenty of work to keep her thoughts at bay.

Well into the evening the phone rang. Though she often worked well into the evening hours, most nights the secretary flipped on the automated answering system when she left, but tonight Alyson had asked her to leave it for her to do just in case her sister or her parents or the detective called. Lunging for the ringing phone and fervently hoping that it was her sister, she almost knocked over the mug of lukewarm coffee on her desk. The voice on the other end was definitely not her sister's. It was Detective Dennison. Recovering from her disappointment, Alyson tried to focus on what he was saying. Since she had yet to hear from her sister and the police search of the area hospitals and shelters had not revealed her whereabouts, they were beginning their search in earnest. He hung up with the promise to go over the details in his office at nine a.m. the following morning.

Alyson sat at her desk long after she had laid the phone back in its cradle. "Alicia where are you?" Alyson asked aloud. Silence was her only answer. Closing her eyes and sitting back in her chair, the frustration she was feeling was being replaced by another feeling. It was the same feeling that she had felt earlier today and still a name to it eluded her. It seemed more than a feeling and knew that she had felt this way even before this morning but could not really recall.

Reality hit and her eyes popped open! What if something terrible had happened to her sister? What if they never saw her again? The thought wedged itself in her mind and she couldn't go on for tears had welled up in her eyes and something felt as if it was constricting her throat? She mentally shook herself and vowed that she would not fall apart. She needed facts. She needed to do something!

Now that she was at home sitting in front of the computer, she generated a duplicate list of all their shared friends, addresses and phone numbers. One of the lists was for herself and one for Detective Dennison. Starting with the first name on the list Alyson began calling to see if someone, anyone had seen or heard from her sister. When she had gone through the entire list, she was still no closer to finding anything factual than when she had begun. Alyson shut down her computer after checking her email.

She took her cup of tea and stood by the window, looking unseeingly into the night, gazing at the stars as if they held the answers that she sought. She knew that something had happened to her sister. She could sense it. Weren't there all kinds of studies documenting that twins possessed an uncanny ability to sense what the other was thinking or feeling? Even though she and her sister weren't identical twins through the years they had demonstrated that such a power was real! Recalling her earliest memory of just such an occurrence, Alyson laughed aloud. She and her sister were in first grade and she had had to stay in for recess (as was and always would be; Alicia the good twin and Alyson the not so good twin) and her arm suddenly began to hurt almost unbearably and she didn't know why until she was told that Alicia had fallen off the jungle gym. Her parents had been called and they all headed to the hospital where x-rays revealed that Alicia had broken her arm in the fall. On the way home, while inspecting the new cast, they had talked and marveled how both had felt the pain of the injury.

Looking about her apartment her gaze settled on the pictures of her family that were arranged on the sofa table. Picking up a picture of her sister that was taken a few months ago, she searched the eyes that were much like her own. "Alicia where are you?" she whispered to the smiling face of her twin, then held the glass frame close to her heart.

"Can you tell me what if anything you've found out so far?" Alyson questioned Detective Dennison the following morning as she took the seat offered to her across the desk from him.

"As I said last night when I spoke to you, the search of the area hospitals didn't turn up anything. Another detective, Louis Willis, is checking the Home Health Agency where she had the meeting that morning. He should be reporting back to me shortly. We'll see what he turns up then proceed from there. We're still looking for the car."

"I can't just sit back and wait! Isn't there anything that I can do?" Alyson asked.

"Let's see. I have a recent photograph of your sister, you've given me a list of her acquaintances, and places she frequents. We've spoken to the people in her office that she works closest with. The only thing I can think of is perhaps you could get with friends and neighbors and circulate her picture using flyers in the area. Sometimes that's been more successful in finding leads to a missing person's whereabouts than anything even we can do. I have to inform you Ms Edwards that we are obligated to give this to the local news media, but we'll need you to sign the necessary papers."

The phone rang and while Dennison attended to it, Alyson sat reading the papers he had handed her. Reality hit hard. Her signature on these papers giving permission to air this story on the local news meant that her sister was really a 'missing person.' Fear gripped her. What if something terrible had happened? What if some insane person had harmed her sister? What if?

Alyson didn't like the path that her thoughts had taken and was glad now that Detective Dennison had finished with his call.

"Ms. Edwards, we've located your sister's car."

Her heart slammed into her chest and her thoughts were momentarily immobilized then immediately jump-started as she tried to focus on what he had just said.

"I'll give you what details we have while we're on the way."

Alyson followed his lead and they weaved their way through the maze of hallways and found themselves in another parking facility. In the car she was able to pull her thoughts from the binding grip of fear to ask, "Where did they find Alicia's car?"

"Ridge State Mountain Park," he answered. "Apparently park officials noticed the vehicle there for the past two days. The park is open only during certain hours and overnight parking is prohibited. They thought the car belonged to one of the caretakers but since it had not been moved for two days they decided to call it in. The description matched the one we have on file for your sister and when we ran a check on the license plate, it was registered to Alicia Edwards."

Her hand flew to her mouth to silence the words that were about to spill forth.

"What is it Ms. Edwards?"

"Was there any sign of my sister?"

"No not yet, but I'm hopeful that this will give us a strong lead in finding her."

Before long they reached the entrance to the park. Alyson had lived in Atlanta most of her life, but never knew this park existed. It was tucked away on the outskirts of Dekalb County. Alyson spotted Alicia's blue Ford Taurus as they rounded the corner that led into the parking facilities. They parked next to two other police cars and a black sedan. The area was blocked off with police tape and the officers were canvassing the area.

Alyson was introduced to Detective Louis Willis, who was a short stocky man with graying hair. He immediately began to fill them in on what information he had.

"There is no evidence that the car has been vandalized. Of course we can't rule out car jacking at this point. It was locked when we found it so we had to jimmy the lock. It's being dusted for fingerprints right now. We'll need to get a search warrant to search her apartment and to dust it for fingerprints also to make sure that the prints we get are a match and if they aren't it'll give us a good starting point. We'll do a thorough search of the car. A search team has been dispatched so that the grounds can be searched also. Robbery doesn't appear to be a factor since her purse was found in the car. It appears to be in tact, but we'll need some information from Ms. Edwards to confirm that."

Alyson noticed the man with the door open on the driver's side busy working. She was trying to take in all of what Detective Willis had said. Her thoughts were racing out of control again. If robbery wasn't the motive, that left a host of other equally horrible ones in it's wake!

"Ms. Edwards we'll need a list of anything you think your sister usually carried in her purse. We'll run a credit check to make sure all her credit cards are here. We'll check the bank to make sure the last check in her checkbook has cleared and at the same time put a stop to her account should any future checks appear. We'll also put a hold on her credit cards for that same reason."

"Mr. Willis is there," Alyson's voice had a strangled sound that she attempted to clear then began again, "Is there any sign of my sister?" Alyson looked into kind eyes.

"I'm sorry Miss. So far we've found no sign of your sister. There is however another possible reason that her car is here. It could have been stolen and then left here when the thief or thieves were finished with it. We'll know more later."

Several more police cars and a van pulled into the parking lot and officers with several dogs joined the small group that was already there. Everyone was led to the nearest pavilion and given orders for the search.

When they dispersed Alyson went back to where Alicia's car was parked. The officer had finished dusting for fingerprints and another was now searching it for content. She watched on in silent disbelief. What could have happened? *How* could this have happened? Didn't this happen to other people not to someone she knew, and certainly not to her own sister. In a city the size of Atlanta and its suburbia, there were oftentimes reports of missing persons aired on the evening news. She saw the faces of the missing and saw the faces of their families never once thinking of the terror and anguish nor of the helplessness they probably felt just as she was feeling now. She had watched them never once thinking that anything like that could happen to her own family.

There were police officers moving about everywhere for the search was well underway now. Alyson took a moment to reign in her emotions and take in her surroundings. There were several covered pavilions each with picnic benches and a grill for cooking. There were other picnic benches sprinkled about. There was a play area for children with a colorful array of swings, slides and jungle gyms. On this spring morning the trees were sporting new leaves and the dogwood trees were in full bloom. She could almost imagine families here on outings laughing and playing. It was a beautiful park. She couldn't understand how her sister or her car had come to be here. She had not known of the parks existence and thinking back was sure her sister had never mentioned it either.

"Ms Edwards I'd like a word with you," Detective Dennison said as he approached her. "The officers are searching the grounds and the car has been dusted for fingerprints. The search team will stay out until dusk." He was checking his watch as he spoke. If they don't find anything then they'll resume the search tomorrow morning.

Just then Alyson heard a shrill whistle and someone yelled out Dennison's name. When both Dennison and Alyson looked in the direction of the sound, Detective Willis was waving his arms in an effort to gain their attention. He was gesturing for them to come where he stood. Alyson's heart began to pick up its rhythmic pace and by the time she reached Willis her heart felt as if it was in her throat.

"The guys have found something," Willis looked at Alyson then addressed Dennison. "This way," he motioned for them to follow him. He turned off the worn path and led them through a thick grove of trees.

Alyson had to will her legs to move and to will her mind to remain blank. Whatever *they* had found, she had to prepare herself to face it. They soon broke free of the thick grove of trees and stood in a small clearing. Other men and two dogs were gathered all in a particular area of the clearing.

"Over here Dennison." One of the men spoke.

When they reached the spot where all the men and dogs had gathered, there was a large white handkerchief on a low-lying bush. Dennison donned gloves and pulled a clear plastic bag from his suit pocket.

Alyson wasn't aware of the gasp that escaped her as she noted the large embroidered initials on one of the corners.

AME embroidered in gold thread. Alicia Marie Edwards.

A wave generated from some place deep within her, threatened to engulf her and submerge her into oblivion. Unseeingly she reached out and grabbed something, anything that would keep her from going under.

"Ms Edwards are you okay? Maybe you should sit down on this rock for a moment."

Willis' voice seemed to come from someplace far away. Alyson willed herself from the void by doggedly focusing on his voice. Her voice was barely above a whisper, "Alicia. It's Alicia's."

With gloved hands and some sort of small instrument, Detective Dennison gingerly picked up the handkerchief and put it in the plastic bag he held in his other hand. Other orders were given out and men and dogs continued their search of the area.

As Alyson sat on a large rock nearby, her thoughts took her back over the past 48 hours. As more and more time passed by, she realized that something was terribly wrong. Why had Alicia been here and when? What if someone had brought her sister here with the intent to harm her? Alyson realized that she had to get a grip on her runaway thoughts. Her sister was the most giving and loving person she knew, but she wasn't naïve. She was aware that you couldn't put your trust in all people for there were people in the world who were not good, and who sought to harm rather than help.

The handkerchief. Their mother had given them both one upon nature's passage into womanhood. Alyson had been first at age thirteen just as she was first born. Alicia had cried because up until that moment, they had done everything together and she had cried every month thereafter until four months later she too received hers. It was Alyson's idea that they form a pact that the handkerchief was to stand as a symbol of the solidarity of their bond as sisters and lifelong friends and that they would always be there for one another through the laughter and the tears for the handkerchief would serve also as the 'crying towel.'

She rummaged through her purse and pulled from it an identical one bearing the initials **ALE**. Alyson Leanna Edwards. She always carried it with her, as did her sister. As long as she could remember Alicia had called her 'Allie' because as a toddler she couldn't quite pronounce Alyson. She ran her fingertips over the thick embroidered letters as a huge tear fell and left its mark on the crisp linen.

She and Alicia had done everything together up until the point of their initiation into womanhood. Things changed from that point on. Though the bond between them remained strong, it was tested from time to time by their individual tug of wars to develop their own personalities. Now as grown women they were the most dissimilar of siblings. Alicia was the good twin while Alyson was the not so good one during their adolescent and young adult years. Alicia was humble, Alyson haughty. Alicia was a peacekeeper, Alyson while not argumentative didn't mind a good debate if the opportunity presented itself. The list of differences stretched into eternity. Alicia possessed an air about her that was ethereal in nature that Alyson secretly envied. It was as if she walked with angels or something. She was heavy into Christianity. Alyson had tried to go with her to church, had tried to embrace the God that her sister put above all else even their relationship, but she couldn't and she knew that her sister felt deep disappointment because of this. Alyson admitted to herself that she had been jealous of His place in her sister's life. Jealous of the love and devotion her sister gave to another above all else.

The search team stayed out all day. Alyson had to return to the hospital. Later Detective Dennison had phoned to say that with the exception of a few footprints near the water's edge, the search had turned up nothing new and that they would resume the search in the morning. A cast had been made of the footprints and it would be taken to the crime lab for further investigation.

Alyson left the office after the phone call with Detective Dennison and drove over to her parents. She needed to be with them when she told them of the events of the day.

She sat them both down while she went over each detail and took great care when she told them about the finding of Alicia's handkerchief. Pushing her own feelings aside Alyson tried to comfort her parents. "Mom, Dad, we'll get through this."

"I know that God will take care of my baby girl." Her mother spoke with a strength that had been proven through the years.

Alyson looked at her mother incredulously! After the ordeal she had been through earlier today, how dare her mother sit there on the sofa hugging one of the pillows and speak as if her God would just make Alicia reappear!

"I know that wherever she is, God is watching over her and no harm will come to her." Her mother spoke again.

Alyson opened her mouth to speak and then closed it on the flood of angry words that where about to rush forth. She looked into her mother's face, her eyes. There was such strength and such courage and something more. Conviction. She truly believed what she was saying. There had long been a silent agreement between them that if they didn't try to force their God on her, she in turn would leave them to their beliefs. Alyson couldn't remain silent this time. Whether it was fatigue or fear or both, she boldly faced her mother. "Mom how can you say that? How can you sit there and say that? Alicia is missing. Where is your God and how could he have allowed this to happen. How can you still believe in a God who would allow this awful thing to happen to Alicia of all people? She loved Him more than her very life!" Alyson was unaware that tears were falling from her mother's eyes for they had clouded her own vision.

Her mother sat down beside her and put her arms around her daughter and they wept together.

"Oh mom, I'm sorry. I didn't mean to hurt you or to make you cry." She was truly sorry.

"Baby I know this all looks so horrible, so awful, but I believe that God is always in charge. I believe that it will be all right and that wherever Alicia is God is there with her keeping her safe." Her mother placed a caressing hand on her daughter's cheek.

"Oh Mom," Alyson said in resignation for she didn't understand now nor had she ever understood the faith that her sister or her mother had in an entity one just had to 'believe' existed.

"Why don't you stay here tonight?" Her mother suggested.

"No mom, I should get back to my place just in case."

Alyson left her parent's with a heavy heart. The moon was full and a million stars twinkled in the night sky. This world was so big. Who would care what happened to one little person. If one little person just disappeared forever, who would know? Who would tell? Who would care?

In the days that followed the park was searched fully, but no new evidence was found. Alyson had flyers printed up with Alicia's face and a phone number as to whom to contact if one had information as to her whereabouts. There was even a substantial reward that Alyson had gotten together with her parents and the hospitals in the area that had ties to where Alicia worked and some that did not. The neighborhood had come out in full strength not only to add to the reward, but also to provide the leg work in distributing the flyers and they talked to anyone and everyone as they did so. The local news stations aired the story continually keeping the community abreast of any new developments. This kept Alicia's face before the public. They had also done a segment of Alyson and her parents pleading for information regarding Alicia, which they aired during prime time.

The days slipped into weeks and the weeks slipped into months and Alyson struggled to bring some semblance of normalcy to her life. Even with all their effort and that of the police, no new evidence was found and what was even worse, no one had come forth with any information that led to her sister. Nobody knew anything. Nobody had seen anything. It was as if her sister had just vanished into thin air!

The Arrival

Caught Up

Chapter 3

Alyson awoke with a start. She hadn't had the dream in a long, long time now.

The area heavy with foliage, the waterfall.

She shook her head to clear it and sat up in bed. She had been dreading this day for weeks now. She had two choices. She could stay here and pull the covers over her face until the day was over or she could get out of bed and carry on as she had this past year.

"A year," she whispered. "Today makes one year." Her sister had been gone for a year now. Tears formed in her eyes. "One more good cry," Alyson spoke to the walls of her bedroom. She had cried more in the past year than she had her whole life. She had had to find a way to deal with the frustration, to deal with the fear, and to now face the reality that she might never see her sister again. Though her mother had held fast to her belief that Alicia was safe somewhere, her faith never wavering in a God that remained silent and gave them no hope, she herself had no such steadfast convictions. Because of her mother, they had kept the lease on her sister's apartment and had garaged her car. Her mother acted as if one day Alicia would just simply walk back into their lives.

Alyson emptied herself of all tears yet again, and resolved to get out of bed and face the day. Since she usually brought work home, her Saturdays were spent working. After she made herself a cup of coffee, she spread the contents of her briefcase on the computer desk with the intent to immerse herself in work, but her mind would not co-operate. She couldn't seem to stay focused on the work at hand.

An hour later, she shut down the computer, showered and dressed in jeans and a tee shirt grabbed her purse and headed for her car.

She had not intended to go anywhere in particular. She just drove. Thoughts of her sister were heavy on her mind and without realizing it she found herself at the entrance to Ridge State Mountain Park. She had not been here since the day they had found her sister's car. She thought of turning around but a car was honking for her to keep moving so she proceeded through the entrance. After finding a parking space, Alyson sat for a long time contemplating her next move. Her choice was to run or confront. She chose to confront, got out, locked her car and walked over to a nearby bench.

The park looked so different today. There were quite a number of people. It really was a beautiful spring day to be out and about. The children's play area was alive with laughing children swinging and sliding with not a care in the world. People were spread out on blankets, while others were cooking on grills underneath covered pavilions. She could smell the tantalizing aroma of grilled meats and barbecue that reminded her that she had not yet eaten.

She still had so many questions, yet there was no one who could answer them for her. Though the police had never found any conclusive evidence that Alicia had actually been here, Alyson believed that a year ago her sister *was* here perhaps even in the place she now sat. Would she ever know what had happened that day?

Alyson could feel a tugging at the hem of her tee shirt. She looked down into large brown eyes.

"Why are you sad?" The large brown eyes asked.

The eyes belonged to a little girl Alyson guessed to be about seven or eight. "I was thinking about someone very special to me."

The little girl who had plopped herself down on the bench beside her spoke again, "My name is Kathy. Well it's really Katherine, but everyone calls me Kathy. What's your name?"

"My name is Alyson. Kathy are you here at the park with anyone?" She'd heard that kids had a tendency to wander off if they weren't watched closely.

"Yes, my Dad. He's over there." Kathy said as she pointed to a covered pavilion that was on the other side of the children's play area.

"Which one is your Dad?"

"See, he's the one with the blue shirt and the black shorts."

Alyson still wasn't sure which man Kathy was referring to since several had on varying degrees of blue shirts and dark shorts, so she just said, "Okay." The little girl kept talking telling Alyson about the kids on the playground, which ones were her friends and which ones she didn't know.

"Kathy didn't I tell you not to talk to strangers?"

Alyson had been looking at the children's play area and had not seen anyone approaching them. When she looked in the direction that the voice had come from, there was a tall man wearing black shorts and a navy tee shirt. The brim of a baseball cap shaded his eyes.

"I know Daddy, but she looked so sad. Alyson this is my Daddy."

"Hi," Alyson spoke to the brim of his hat. She watched as he pushed the hat back from his forehead and she could feel his eyes looking her over. He was probably trying to decide if she was a friend or foe! One couldn't be too careful these days especially when a child was involved.

He then extended his hand.

"My name is Darrell Henderson."

"Alyson Edwards." She extended her hand, which was immediately enveloped in a strong handshake. One can tell a lot about another person by the simple act of shaking hands. For instance, if the grasp is weak, then it usually means the person is insecure or not to be trusted. If they only seem to graze the hand, barely shaking it at all, it usually means they think themselves more highly than the person they are greeting. But if the handshake is firm and the eye contact is unwavering, it usually means the person is self-confident and secure in who they are. Darrell Henderson was definitely the latter.

"Kathy they're getting ready to play softball, we'll need to be getting back," Darrell Henderson spoke to his daughter.

"Daddy can Alyson come with us?" Kathy asked her father in all innocence.

Alyson was completely taken off guard by the little girls request and judging by the expression that flashed across her father's face, so was he.

"Please Daddy," Kathy said in that little girls voice that dragged out the word please.

Her father looked at her and smiled then he looked at Alyson.

"Oh no, I wouldn't want to intrude. I just came out for a little fresh air. I still have a ton of work waiting for me." Alyson found herself babbling on, not really knowing why.

"Just for a little while?" Kathy was looking at her with those big brown eyes.

"Really, you wouldn't be intruding," Darrell Henderson put in. "Our church is having our annual picnic. There's plenty of food and fun." He looked at her with eyes similar to his daughter's.

"Are you sure?" Alyson didn't want to crash someone else's good time with her own unhappy thoughts.

"Positive," he said.

On that note she joined Darrell and Kathy Henderson and the Greater Mount Moriah Missionary Baptist Church for their annual picnic.

There were softball games first for the kids then the adult teams were chosen and Darrell talked her into playing. She couldn't remember how long it had been since she had played. Someone tossed her a glove and sent her to second base. The game was fun. There was as much teasing and joking as there was game intensity. In the end, Alyson's team lost to the team Darrell was on by two runs. By the time the game was over, it seemed as if Alyson's sadness had dissipated with the heat of the day.

Darrell insisted that she go with them to the pavilion that the church had claimed theirs for the day for drinks and refreshments.

Alyson laughed to herself when she got to the pavilion and saw for herself his definition of 'refreshments'. The food table was laden with barbecue ribs, chicken, hot links, potato salad, pasta salad, green salad, baked beans, green beans, corn on the cob, and several kinds of rolls. There were cakes, pies and cookies at the end of the table.

Alyson, plate piled high no thanks to Darrell who kept piling it on, sat down with him and his daughter under the pavilion. She had learned the names of some of the other members as they played. Darrell had also introduced her to his pastor and the pastor's wife.

"What would you like to drink? There are chilled sodas, juice and water." Darrell asked her.

"If there's and orange soda, I'll take that," Alyson said.

"Get me one too Daddy!" Kathy said.

All afternoon Alyson kept waiting for a Mrs. Henderson to join them. As of yet she had not materialized. Alyson had long since noted that Darrell Henderson wore no ring on the third finger of his left hand, but one couldn't rule out married or not because of any number of valid reasons.

They ate their fill while exchanging small talk between mouthfuls of food. After they finished eating, Darrell suggested a walk and Alyson readily agreed. A walk would be just the right thing after all the food she had consumed! Looking around for Kathy, Alyson noticed that she had joined a group of girls and they were playing a game of twister.

She and Darrell headed for one of the many walking trails and for a long moment neither spoke.

"I want to thank you for including me today." Alyson was the first to speak.

"No problem," he said smoothly. "I hope you had fun."

"I sure did," Alyson said truthfully, surprised that it was so.

"I don't mean to get all in your business, or maybe I do," he said turning to face her. "Kathy said she went over to talk to you earlier because you looked sad. Would you like to talk about it? I'm a good listener."

They had stopped in front of a large oak tree. Alyson looked into brown eyes that held such warmth and gentleness in them that she found herself telling him, sharing her sadness and her pain.

"And today makes a year to the day," Alyson finished.

"I'm sorry. I can tell this isn't easy for you to talk about."

"No it isn't," Alyson said surprised that she had talked about it for after all he was a stranger to her. "We were, we *are* very close." She corrected her error.

For a long moment there was silence, not an awkward one as she thought there would be, but a companionable one. They started walking again. They talked about family, his and hers. She learned that the picnic was an annual event, but this was the first year it had been held here at this particular park. She learned that his wife had died of breast cancer several years earlier and he and Kathy lived here in Dekalb County. He was a 'suit guy' at IBM, with a double masters in computer science and business and that he had climbed the executive ladder quickly and at thirty-six was one of the top executives in his field. She shared with him her own professional scenario. They seemed to possess similar drive and ambition. Their walk brought them back to the pavilion where they had dessert.

Looking at her watch, Alyson was astonished that the day had just flown by. It was almost five o'clock! "I really should be going now. I still have a ton of work waiting for me."

Darrell and Kathy walked her to her car after she had thanked the leader of his church for the hospitality that they had extended to a stranger.

"Thank you both for inviting me," She looked at Kathy then at her father.

"It was our pleasure," Darrell said.

"Alyson will you come to church with us tomorrow?" Kathy asked.

Alyson was taken aback. She hadn't gone to church in years. She looked at Kathy then at her father.

"Yes, we'd like it if you would join us for service tomorrow," he said with no apparent reserve.

Alyson didn't know what to say. "I'll try. Well thanks again."

She got into her car and with one last wave and a smile she pulled out of the parking lot. A check of her rear view mirror revealed that Darrell and Kathy were still standing where she had left them, watching her retreating car.

She had dreaded the arrival of this day for weeks and yet to her amazement it had turned out to have a truly bright spot in it. Her thoughts returned to a little girl and her father. They were nice people. They had even invited her to their church. She knew that she would not go. She knew that she would probably not see them again. Alyson laughed to herself. This was as close she had come to a date with a man since... She was unable to continue her line of thinking for a flood of unexpected tears clogged her throat and welled over the brim of her eyes clouding her vision.

Alyson pulled over onto the shoulder of the road. The wave of pain that assaulted her doubled her over the steering wheel and in great heaves, she wept. "Oh Alicia," she said gulping for air as wave upon wave threatened to pull her under to a depth of total despair in which she feared she would never be able to emerge from. She wept for all that was precious, her memories of a sister that was not just her sister but was her best friend. There was so much they had not gotten to do together; so much she hadn't gotten to say to her. She wept for she was afraid that there would never be another moment together with her sister now or ever.

Alyson didn't know how long she sat in her car on the shoulder of the road, but her tears were now spent and the waves of pain were only a remnant of their previous intensity. Her face marred by trails of streaked mascara and eyes red and swollen, she sat emotionally exhausted.

Alyson pulled into her parent's drive way. She checked her reflection in the mirror to assure herself that the outward signs of her earlier distraught emotions were not visible. She had stopped at a small store and after several minutes with an ice pack, she washed her face, applied new mascara, face powder and a touch of lipstick. She let herself into the house with her key and found her parents in the living room watching old videos of the family when she and her sister were little girls. Her parents had not seemed to notice that she had come into the house let alone the room for they seemed transfixed to the big screen television that occupied a corner of the room. She watched as she and Alicia frolicked on the beach, posing for the camera and giggling uncontrollably when their father ran up and grabbed both girls one under each arm and ran into the water. They had gone to Florida on vacation that year. Their parents had surprised them with a trip to Disney World. Alyson still standing in the entrance, watched as the video moved from the beach to scenes at Disney World; rides and poses with Mickey and Minnie Mouse and Goofy.

When the video came to an end no one moved, no one spoke. They just remained where they were staring at the blank screen.

"Mom, Dad." Alyson said softly so as not to startle them.

"Alyson we didn't hear you come in." Her mother got up and came over to hug her hard. "It's so good to see you," she said in her ear.

For a long moment they just hugged one another taking comfort from the very physical presence of the other.

"How's my girl?" Her Dad came over and hugged her solidly.

"Just fine Dad." Alyson managed a weak smile. She knew that he knew better. Whoever said that little boys belong to their mothers and little girls belong to their fathers, knew what they were talking about! She and Alicia had definitely been Daddy's little girls.

"How are you doing Dad?"

"Oh baby, just hanging in there," he said as he patted her back and held her to him.

This was home. With her family around her, she felt safe in the arms of their unconditional love for one another.

Alyson watched as her father retreated to his favorite place to bear his pain in silence. Her father was a quiet man who loved his family fiercely. She followed her mother into the kitchen and watched as she pulled one loaf of bread out of the oven and began kneading another. There was nothing like the smell of bread baking in the oven. The smell permeated every wall in the house inviting one to familiarity and comfort. They had always been a bread loving family.

Alyson remembered that a few years ago she had bought her mother one of those automatic bread machines. Her mother had put her hand against her cheek lovingly and said, "Baby I appreciate your thinking of me, but I can tell you now that this is one gift I know I'll never use so I don't want you wasting your money." Alyson remembered that her feelings had been hurt for the bread machine had not turned out to be the perfect gift as she had hoped, until her mother helped her understand.

"Honey, I don't just bake bread because we like it, I do it because it keeps me focused even grounded at times. There's nothing like kneading a loaf of bread. That's the best therapy I know." Then she laughed and said, "Besides, I have a feeling you could use this little gem yourself!"

"As long as I can come home and eat bread in this kitchen, I doubt I'll be making any myself." Alyson had laughed. She had returned the bread machine and bought tickets for her mother to the ballet. Alyson watched as her mother shaped the bread dough into a loaf, placed it into the waiting pan and then into the oven.

"Come on baby and have a seat, I know your mouth is just watering for a slice while its still warm," her mother said.

They sat at the table eating warm bread spread with strawberry butter and drinking coffee, chatting about everything except the thing they both yearned to talk about. Alyson told her about being at the park earlier, omitting why.

"So is he nice?" Her mother asked with more than just curiosity in her voice.

"He seems to be though I couldn't say for certain since I only just met him today and probably won't ever see him again."

"You're not planning to see him again?"

"No Mom. The last thing I need is a man in my life!" Alyson took note of her mother's raised eyebrow and added, "Let me clarify that even further. The last thing I need is a man and an eight-year-old child in my life. Besides he's really not my type."

"And what is your type?" Her mother gently inquired.

Alyson thought for a moment. "I don't know, but when I meet him I'm sure I'll know," she said as she grimaced at her mother for putting her on the spot that way.

"I thought you said he was a nice guy," her mother said teasingly.

"I'm not going to see him again, end of discussion. Now lets just change the subject!" The moment the words left her lips Alyson regretted them for the mood instantly changed from pseudo-jovial to solemn. "I miss her so much Mom," Alyson spoke just above a whisper as her voice caught with emotion.

Her mother reached across the table and grasped her daughter's hand. "You know there are times that I catch myself dialing her phone number. There are even times when I can hear her voice. I think I must be losing my mind," her mother attempted to lighten the mood, but her laughter held no humor.

"I can hear her voice at times too. I miss her so much." Alyson could see the sadness in her mother's eyes. "Mom each day that passes eats away my hope that we'll ever see Alicia again. It's been a year Mom, a whole year and the worst part is we still don't have a clue as to what happened. We don't know if she's okay or not."

She couldn't bring herself to say the words, dead or alive. "We have nothing but this terrible void. How Mom? How could this have happen?"

"Honey I don't have any answers, but I know that God has the answers. My prayer group and the whole church have been sending up prayers. I know we don't understand, but I know that we will know by and by."

"Oh Mom!" Alyson was incredulous that after all this time her mother still held fast to belief in her God. A God that seemed not to care that she was suffering due to the loss of a child.

"Do you know that Darrell and Kathy invited me to their church tomorrow? Church and God and religion, that's your thing Mom not mine. It was Alicia's thing too and look what happened!" Alyson hadn't meant to vent her frustration on her mother. They both felt sad enough as it was.

"My prayer has always been that God would send His angels to watch over my girls. I don't have any answers. I just know that God has never failed me. No, He never has."

Her mother got up from the table to check the loaf in the oven.

She turned from the oven to face her daughter the pain and longing evident in her eyes. "Honey, just give God a chance. I know it looks and feels bad right now, but I know that He has the answer and that He will answer our prayers."

Alyson just nodded, her only admission to solemn defeat in an argument that she would never win against her mother and the God she spoke so highly of. She hugged her mother tightly and whispered, "I love you" and then left her mother standing at the oven and went in search of her father.

She found him in the garden, his haven, among the roses. His garden was the envy of the neighborhood. Now that he was retired, he spent a large part of his day doing what he loved.

"They're gorgeous Dad!" Alyson bent down to smell a large fragrant yellow rose, then took a seat in the garden swing beside him. With one foot he gently set in motion the swing and Alyson laid her head on his shoulder. "Dad I worry about you." She expressed her thoughts aloud.

"No need to honey." He said patting her hand.

"Do you remember when we were little and we hurt ourselves playing? You would patch us up, give us a peppermint and send us on our way."

"Uh huh," he replied simply ever so gently swaying the swing.

"How do I pick myself up Dad. How do I go on from here? I'm completely lost." Her head on his shoulder felt a drop of moisture fall to her cheek and looking up she was taken aback. Her father was crying. Her father was a man of few words but he exuded a confidence and a strength born out of pulling oneself up successfully in hard times. "Oh Daddy," Alyson turned slightly and put her arms around the man who had always been the strong pillar in her life, bearing her up through the years.

"I've lost one of my babies, one of my little girls. Someone has taken her away from us and there wasn't anything I could do about it. Nothing!" He just kept saying nothing! Nothing! Nothing!

They sat in the garden on a spring evening, the wind swaying the swing, being comforted by the familiar presence of the other.

Later that night Alyson lay in bed in her apartment thinking about the day. She had not wanted to face it. She thought of her struggle against despair and hopelessness. She thought of her sadness and mourned the bond that had been severed abruptly. Then her thoughts turned to a little girl and her father who had included her in their lives for a few hours and in taking her mind off herself and her loss, she had been able to get through the day. She had actually had a pleasant time even if for a short while. She would never forget their kindness. She doubted that she would ever see them again since she had no intention of going to their church in the morning or any Sunday morning.

Chapter 4

The days that followed took on their usual pattern. Alyson worked hard all day and brought home more work to escape the pain of her loss. Returning from work one Monday evening, Alyson checked her messages. She listened as her mother reminded her of the plans they had made to go shopping, the dentist office confirming an appointment for the following Tuesday and a voice she hadn't heard in a long while.

"Hey Girl, it's me. Surprise! I'll be in town on Wednesday for a conference. I'd rather bunk at your place than a hotel so I've taken the liberty of inviting myself, you know, so we can catch up on all the old news and any fresh news. Don't worry about picking me up from the airport, I know the way!" The last part was hurried with the end of the recording time close on its heels.

Alyson laughed. Shelly! Nobody but Shelly would take the liberty of not booking a hotel and assume that she had nothing better to do than be at her beck and call! She laughed again.

It had been at least two years since she'd seen her friend from college. In their freshman year of college the dormitory had overbooked the number of occupants and Shelly had had to stay in their room until they had secured her a permanent room. They all had become good friends and the following semester had shared a suite that could accommodate them all comfortably. They remained roommates throughout college. Since graduation they hadn't gotten to see each other much. Shelly had taken a job with a major computer firm that had international ties and she spent a lot of time out of the country. Yes, they had a lot of catching up to do. In the meantime she had a lot of work to catch up on as usual.

On Wednesday morning while Alyson sat at her desk, which was piled high with folders and files, the remnants of lunch now discarded, the door burst open.

"Hey girl. I knew I'd find you here. I didn't see your secretary, so I took the liberty of showing myself in."

Alyson looked up from the file she was reviewing and laughed. "Shelly! You never did have any manners!" She fondly teased her friend as she got up and gave her a big welcoming hug.

"I should be offended, but coming for you I'll make an exception," Shelly said as she laughed good-naturedly. How long has it been anyway? Let me look at you. "Uh hum," she said speculatively.

"What do you mean by uh hum," Alyson said to her friend.

"That means you're getting those age furrows in your forehead."

"What are you talking about? I'm as youthful as I was when we were in college," Alyson said with a mock scowl on her face.

"Girl who are you fooling? We're all getting old!"

"At thirty-two you might be old, but I haven't even reached my prime!" Alyson hugged her friend and they both laughed again. "Have a seat," Alyson said to her friend, motioning for her to join her on the sofa in her office.

"How long has it been anyway?"

"It's been at least two years according to my calculations," Alyson said.

"Yeah, two years too long! So out with it and don't you leave out one single solitary detail of your life since I last saw you."

"Speaking of details, if you didn't change your address every six months, maybe we'd be able to keep in touch like we promised," Alyson admonished her friend.

"Okay, okay, that was a cheap shot!" Shelly responded with a broad smile. "You know it's the hazards of the job!"

"You know you love it. The traveling, the quick pace, the demand for your highness, you thrive on it!" Alyson had so missed her friend.

"Yes I do. I admit it. I love every bit of it!" Shelly punctuated each sentence with laughter. "Now let's get back to business. Oh, before I forget, guess who I ran into in Cancun a few months ago?"

"I couldn't even begin to guess," Alyson answered, not bothering to hide her envy at the mention of Cancun.

"Carl Hill," Shelly said dragging the name out.

"Carl Hill!" Alyson repeated in disbelief.

"Yes according to him, he was there to 'clear his head.' Apparently he and his wife just got a divorce. He asked about you and Alicia and wondered what had happened to you both."

At the mention of Alicia's name, Alyson's thoughts wavered from the conversation. She realized that Shelly didn't know, couldn't know that her sister was...

"Alyson are you okay?"

Alyson's thoughts were halted as Shelly's voice called her back from the past to the present. "Shelly there's something I need to tell you." She hesitated then plunged right in. "Alicia is gone."

"Gone," Shelly inquired not comprehending the scope of that one little spoken word.

"Missing," Alyson tried to clarify *missing*. She's been missing for over a year now."

"Missing! What happened?"

Alyson could tell from the look on Shelly's face that she was still having difficulty comprehending what 'missing' meant. "We don't know what happened. I spoke with her on the morning that she disappeared. I didn't hear anything more after that. Her car was found at a local park, but we still don't know how it came to be there."

"You mean," Shelly began but stopped.

"I mean we don't know if she drove it there of if someone else drove it there although only Alicia's fingerprints were found in the car." Alyson tried hard to maintain her composure.

"Oh Alyson," Shelly hugged her close. "Why didn't you call me? I could have at least been there for you."

"I was so distraught I guess it just slipped my mind." Alyson took comfort from talking to her old friend again.

"Oh Alyson," Shelly said again. "How are your parents holding up through all this?"

"You know Mom," Alyson said pulling back from her friend to stand in front of her desk. "She's as solid as a rock and hoping for a miracle from her God. She thinks that one day her little girl is just going to reappear and walk right back into our lives." Alyson didn't try to mask her bitterness.

"And your Dad?"

"He doesn't say much, but I know it's tearing him apart inside." Alyson could feel his pain just as acutely as she felt her own. "Shelly you know what's the worst part of all this?" She didn't care that tears were building up to overflowing and she didn't wait for Shelly to answer. "The worst part is the *not knowing*. If there was a body, we could at least have some closure, but we have nothing. Nothing. It's as if she just walked away into thin air, which is ludicrous because no one just walks away into thin air," Alyson said.

"Oh girl, I wish I had known," Shelly said trying to keep her own emotions in check, so that she could be strong for her friend.

"Hey, how was old Carl anyway," Alyson said in an effort to lift the heaviness of the moment.

"Finer than ever," Shelly said taking Alyson's unspoken lead.

"Fine huh," Alyson said, smiling through the mist of tears.

"Yeah, you know I never did understand why one of you didn't marry that man when we graduated."

"Marry him!" Alyson laughed out loud. "Probably because he couldn't make up his mind if he wanted me or my sister!"

Shelly laughed with her. "I've got to go check in and make sure my registration is okay at the conference hall. Things don't get underway until tomorrow morning. I'll meet you back here at five o'clock so no working late for you tonight. We'll have dinner out and since it's my treat, I get to choose the place." Shelly winked broadly at Alyson as she rose to leave. "We'll have plenty of time to catch up while we have a long leisurely dinner."

After Shelly left, Alyson sat at her desk thinking about her conversation with Shelly. What if Alicia *had* been the one to marry Carl Hill? If a person could change one aspect of the past, wouldn't it skew the whole outcome? If so then Alicia would be here today. Wouldn't she? Alyson mentally shook herself. There was no way of knowing that, not now. Not ever.

Alyson wasn't surprised when Shelly pulled her rented car up in front of 'Little Italy.' It was Shelly's favorite and whenever she was in town, she had to eat there. It boasted the most exquisite Italian cuisine this side of the Atlantic. Alyson looked at her friend and laughed.

"Don't give me that look!" Shelly returned the laughter. "You knew I'd choose Little Italy. It's the best!"

Since Shelly had made reservations, they didn't have to wait for a table. The waiter returned shortly with their drink order and a loaf of hot bread and a small plate of herbs in olive oil for dipping the bread.

"This is wonderful. I haven't been here since the last time you were in town," Alyson said as she helped herself to a slice of warm bread.

"It's a good thing I don't live here in Atlanta, I'd eat here every night! The bread alone would probably be my undoing," Shelly said as she closed her eyes in order to savor every bite.

During the course of the evening they caught up on one another's lives.

"Still trying to be the movers and the shakers of this world, that's us and still alone!" Shelly said with no apparent hint at being lonely.

Alyson felt someone tap her on the shoulder and turning slightly she saw a familiar face. "Kathy," she exclaimed in surprise!

"Hi Alyson."

"Hi yourself," Alyson returned. "My don't you look very pretty and quite the little lady," Alyson said taking in her freshly done hair pulled back into a ponytail of crisp ringlet curls and her pretty peach colored dress.

"Thank you," Kathy said, smiling broadly.

"Forgive my manners. Kathy I'd like you to meet a good friend of mine, Shelly Green." Alyson watched as Kathy reached to shake the hand that Shelly held out to her.

"Pleased to meet you." Kathy said.

"Likewise," Shelly said.

"Kathy, who are you here with?" Alyson inquired.

"I'm here with my Dad." Kathy said. "It's my birthday and were celebrating. He said he chose a more grown-up place this year since I'm not such a baby anymore, but between you and me,

I'd much rather eat at Chuckie Cheese," she smiled dimples deepening both cheeks.

"Where's your dad sweetie?" Alyson asked.

"He's over there," Kathy said as she pointed to a table on the other side of the room and motioned for him to come and join them.

Three pairs of eyes watched as Darrell Henderson strode across the room.

"Good evening ladies," he said when he arrived.

"Good evening," Alyson and Shelly said in unison.

"Darrell Henderson, I'd like you to meet a good friend of mine, Shelly Green," Alyson made the introduction as Shelly accepted his outstretched hand. "Won't you join us?" Alyson invited.

"No thank you, we're just about to leave. We've had dinner and dessert," he said.

"The waiters brought out a birthday cake with candles and ice cream and they sang 'Happy Birthday' to me," Kathy said excitedly. "Look what Daddy gave me," she said eyes glowing with pride as she showed Alyson the charm bracelet that her daddy had given her.

"It's very beautiful. Happy birthday," Alyson said inspecting the small arm that was stretched out in front of her.

"Thank you," Kathy said.

"Well we should be going," Darrell said. "It was nice to have met you Shelly and it was good seeing you again Alyson," he said, holding Alyson's gaze.

Kathy said goodbye and Alyson watched as they left the restaurant. When she turned her attention back to Shelly, she found her just staring at her. "What?" She asked feigning naivety.

"What do you mean 'what?' It appears that somebody's been holding out on me." Shelly playfully accused her.

"What do you mean holding out on you?" Alyson tried to sound indignant but failed.

"I'll refresh your memory. Let's begin with Mr. Tall, gorgeous and obviously available! Now out with it and don't you leave out any of the details." Shelly admonished her friend.

"There's really not much to tell. A couple of months ago, I went back to the park where the police found Alicia's car. I was deep in thought when this little girl came up to me and started talking to me. Her father came over a short while later and invited me to join them and their church for their annual picnic and I did. I had a wonderful time. It really helped to take my mind off things for a while. When the day was over they invited me to join them at church the following day and I left. End of story!" Alyson finished hurriedly already aware that Shelly was reading more into this than was necessary if the expectant look on her face was anything to go by.

"Well did you?" Shelly asked with no intention of letting Alyson off the hook.

"Did I what?" Alyson tried not to make eye contact.

"See him again, go to church, anything!" Shelly questioned her relentlessly.

"No I did not see him again at least not until tonight," Alyson answered and sent Shelly a look that warned her not to continue with her line of questioning.

"You mean you haven't so much as called, or even e-mailed a man who is obviously interested in seeing you?" Shelly scolded her friend.

"No I have not and what do you mean by obviously interested in seeing me?" Alyson probed.

"Girl, I saw the way that man was gazing at you."

"He was not 'gazing' at me." Alyson pretended to be upset.

"You are in denial." Shelly said as her eyes lit up and a slow smile spread across her face. "You're scared aren't you?"

"I never could hide anything from you." Alyson said not bothering to hide the annoyance in her voice.

"Admit it," Shelly said and sent her a look that said 'I dare you.'

"Okay, okay, I'm scared. You got it out of me, now are you happy?" Alyson stuck her tongue out at her friend. She knew it was childish but she didn't care.

"Happy, overjoyed and extremely ecstatic!" Shelly said as she sat back in her chair. "I wish *you* were happy my friend," Shelly said her tone more serious.

"I *am* happy. I have a job that I love, where I feel as if I'm making a difference in people's lives. I have my family and friends. What more could a girl want?" Alyson ended her little speech just a little too defiant.

"How about someone to share your life with, someone to hold your hand when you're scared, to comfort you when you're hurting, to support your dreams, share your concerns, to be a wife and a mother?"

Alyson's eyes grew wide. "Wait a minute," she said putting her hands up in front of her in an effort to stop the onslaught of insanity coming from the other side of the table. "Speak for yourself!"

"We are not talking about me, we are talking about you." Shelly put the emphases on the word we. "I am not the marrying kind. My philosophy has always been and still is love um and leave um. But you on the other hand are a loving and giving and nurturing woman. *Definitely* the marrying kind! Besides, I saw how you watched him and his daughter a moment ago. Don't think I didn't notice. Close your mouth and stop staring at me!"

Alyson was not aware that she had been staring at her friend with her mouth open in astonishment. She gathered her scattered wits. "I deny everything you just said. Besides, this man comes with an eight-year old child. I don't know the first thing about being somebody's wife let alone somebody's mother."

"Shall we take a walk down memory lane?" Shelly extended the invitation smugly. "Do you remember sophomore year when we both got jobs at that daycare on campus? You took the two year olds and I took the four-year olds whom I thought would be more mature and therefore easier to handle? Boy was I ever wrong! They were little darlings one moment and a terror to behold the next! One week at that place and I knew I wasn't cut out to be a mother! When I put them down for their nap, I would sneak down the hall and peak into your room. The shades would be drawn with soft lullaby music playing in the background and you would be reading a story in a hushed tone with one of those little ones fast asleep on you lap. I thought to myself as I looked at you, Alyson's going to be a great mother someday!"

Alyson allowed her mind to conjure up memories of that time and thoughts of excitedly rushing from class to get to her job at the daycare came forth. The kids were always just as excited to see her as she had been to see them. Thinking back, it was the best job she had ever had with the exception of the one she now had of course. "Yeah that was fun." Alyson conceded.

"Speak for yourself!" Shelly said. "You kept that job for two years. On the other hand, I lasted three weeks and was glad to find another job at Joe's Pizzeria. Now that was more my style!"

"Kathy isn't exactly two you know. She's practically all grown up. How am I supposed to relate to an eight year old?" Alyson looked at Shelly and rolled her eyes upward.

"You have to start by first not turning down the offer to get to know one another better. Open the door and the rest will take care of itself." Shelly counseled her friend.

Long after she and Shelly had turned in for the night, Alyson lay awake in bed, thinking back over the evening. She was completely happy with the way her life had progressed, at least with the exception of her sister's disappearance. Her career was on track. Sure there was no man in her life but she didn't feel empty because of that. But maybe Shelly had a point too. What could be the harm in just getting to know Darrell and his daughter? It certainly didn't mean that she was duty bound to marry him by just accepting an invitation to spend some time together. On that note she switched off the bedside light and resolved to call him.

The following afternoon after calling her mother to warn her that she and Shelly would be showing up for dinner, Alyson sat at her desk staring down at the business card that Darrell had given her before they had parted on the day of the picnic. Twice she had dialed the pager number only to hang up before completing the task. "Third time's a charm," she thought as she finally completed her mission. What would she say to him if he responded to her page? She was absolutely clueless. "Come on Alyson, you've undauntedly confronted the board of directors of the hospital on many occasions. Surely one man and a child should be a piece of cake in comparison!" Alyson said, giving herself the much needed pep talk. Still, her heart jolted when the phone rang a short time later and her hand shook slightly when she picked it up.

"Hello, this is Alyson Edwards," she said as her professional façade came to her rescue.

"Hello Alyson this is Darrell Henderson. The number on the pager was unfamiliar to me. I must say though that I am pleasantly surprised."

Alyson noted the deep resonance of his voice and was glad he couldn't see her blushing at this moment.

"What can I do for you?" Darrell asked.

"I was wondering if you and Kathy would join me for dinner on Friday night," Alyson said in a rush before she lost her nerve.

"We would be honored. Just name the time and the place and we'll be there."

"How about my place at seven o'clock?"

"Sounds great!"

"Good, I'll see you then," Alyson said with a self-assurance she was far from feeling. She gave him her address and her phone number at home in case something came up and he needed to postpone.

After hanging up the phone though she found herself in a state of panic. "What had she done?" She asked herself. "Was she crazy?" So what if society says it's okay to ask a man on a date, it certainly was a deviation from the rules of dating she had set for her own life. Oh well, she threw her hands up! The deed was done and she was not going to call him back and cancel, so she began making a list of the things she needed to purchase in preparation for their dinner on Friday night.

True to their word, she and Shelly landed on her parent's doorstep promptly at six p.m. Her parents rushed them into the house in a flurry of hugs and kisses. They had always treated Shelly like she was part of the family.

Alyson had been laughing so hard at one of Shelly's recent antidotes that her side was aching. It was good being with her old friend again. She had forgotten how much fun they use to have together. She couldn't remember the last time she had laughed so much. The mirth continued on through dinner as Shelly recanted countless tales of her adventurous life. After dinner the girls cleaned up and all retired to the family room for coffee.

Shelly stopped in front of a photograph of herself, Alyson and Alicia that was hanging on the wall amidst several other family pictures. "It's always meant so much to me that you all adopted me after my parents passed away." Shelly said.

"We sure do miss her," Alyson's mother said as she went to stand beside Shelly.

"Yes, Alyson told me what happened. I wish that I had known so that I could have been here for you," Shelly said as she embraced Mrs. Edwards.

"But you know what I believe?" Mrs. Edwards said and not waiting for an answer continued. "I believe that wherever Alicia is she is safe and happy and that God is taking care of her and that we will know someday what really happened."

"Oh mother not that again!" Alyson said trying hard not to be annoyed with her mother.

"I can feel it in my spirit," her mother continued.

Alyson watched as Shelly hugged her mother again. In a determined effort not to spoil the evening, Alyson forced a smile. "I have an announcement to make!" When she was sure she had everyone's attention, she burst out "I have a date! I've invited Darrell and his daughter to dinner at my place on Friday evening."

"Atta girl!" from Shelly.

"Oh that's wonderful!" from her mother.

"About time!" from her father. "It would be good for you to find a nice young man. Maybe even settle down with," he said.

Alyson looked at her father in surprise but before she could respond, her mother and Shelly began their interrogation.

"What are you going to wear? Make sure it knocks him off his feet," Shelly said.

"What are you going to serve? Make sure it makes his mouth water every time he remembers it," her mother said.

"Wait a minute. Hold on, I can see the conspiracy here you guys. Read my lips, this is just dinner not a wedding!"

"It's a beginning!" said Shelly.

"Yes it's a beginning," said Alyson, not bothering to hide the smile that lit her eyes.

She and Shelly soon left pretty much as they had arrived in a flurry of hugs, kisses and promises to keep in touch. Alyson had a full menu of what to serve for Friday night's dinner courtesy of her mother's vast cooking library. Just thinking about it made *her* mouth water!

$\diamond\!\!-\!\!\diamond$ *FB* $\diamond\!\!-\!\!\diamond$

Chapter 5

The week flew by. Shelly left that Thursday but not before extracting a promise that Alyson would call her on the week-end so that she could get the scoop on everything that happened with Friday's date.

That Friday Alyson left work a little early so that she would have time to get everything ready and take a soothing hot bath. By 6:55 p.m. dinner was finished, the appetizers were in the warmer and Alyson dressed in a simple but elegant light blue pant suit, took yet another moment to check her make-up and to take off the apron she was wearing. At 7:00 p.m. sharp the doorbell rang and with it her heart skipped a beat. "My goodness, steady girl, if I didn't know any better, I'd think you were going out on your first date ever!"

"Hi Alyson," Kathy said when she opened the door.

"Hi to you too."

"It's so cool that you've invited us to dinner," Kathy said as she breezed past Alyson leaving her father in the open doorway.

"Hello Darrell."

"Hello Alyson. These are for you." He said as he handed her a bouquet of fresh flowers.

"Thank-you," Alyson said pleased by his thoughtfulness. "Won't you come in? Dinner's ready."

After getting her guest seated, Alyson served the appetizers, stuffed mushroom caps, and took her seat at the small round glass top table in the dining area.

Darrell suggested they say grace and they joined hands as he led them in a prayer of thanksgiving. Alyson thought how very nice this all felt.

"Oh, I love these!" Kathy exclaimed. "Daddy lets me order these when we go out to eat sometimes. Daddy likes them too. Don't you Daddy?"

"I must admit, they are my favorite," Darrell said as he put several on his plate and popped one in his mouth.

Alyson tried to gauge his reaction wondering if hers measured up to his previous taste experience.

"These are wonderful! Much better than any I've tasted at a restaurant. My compliments to the chef!" He smiled at Alyson.

"I'm glad you like them." Alyson said allowing her pleasure at his response to shine in her eyes. "I can't take all the credit. It's my mother's recipe. She's a fabulous cook. She even makes her own bread by hand from scratch!"

"I'm impressed." Darrell said as he finished off the mushrooms on his plate.

Everything was perfect. The salmon was grilled just right; served with dill butter, fresh vegetables, hot buttered rolls, a tossed green salad and cool, tall glasses of lemonade. After dinner, Alyson turned on the computer so that Kathy could play a new computer game she had just installed and she and Darrell moved to the sofa so that they could talk comfortably.

"Nice place you have here," Darrell said.

"Thanks. I've been here a couple of years. Lately though I've been thinking about buying a house."

"With all the new subdivisions going up everyday, you should have a wide variety to choose from. Are you modern, contemporary, traditional or Victorian?" Darrell asked.

"Contemporary, but not too much so. I'd say with a touch of traditional," she answered. "Actually I like a little of each but not to the extreme." She laughed at her own indecisiveness about décor choices.

"Excuse me. Alyson who is the lady in this picture?"

Alyson hadn't noticed that Kathy had left the computer and was standing near the sofa table. Her gaze was directed to the picture in question.

"That's my sister, Alicia. Remember I was telling you about her the day we met in the park?"

"Yes, I remember." Kathy said as she continued to study the picture, forehead wrinkled in deep concentration. "She's very pretty."

"Yes she is." Alyson said determined not to sound wistful. "Well can I get you two anything else to drink?"

"Not a thing." Alyson are you okay?" Darrell asked as he took her hands in his own.

"Yes, yes I am. It's just that it's still a sensitive subject for me. There are times when I think that I've gotten past the emotional part and then something really quite simple will happen like a memory flash of the two of us together, we were always together, or I'll see someone that reminds me of her not so much physically but there will be some gesture or facial expression and it all comes back to me, like the day they found her car and the days that followed." In the short silence that followed Alyson pulled herself back from that place of pain and focused instead on how nice it felt, her hands clasped in his. She noted the texture of his skin and the gentle strength in his grasp. Yes it was nice and so was he. There was something about him that encouraged her to share her joy and her pain and even her fears. He really was a good listener.

"Alyson I know that we haven't known each other long but I want you to know that if you should ever need to talk to someone, day or night, you can call me."

Alyson could see the earnestness in his eyes. "Thank you. I'd like that." They sat hand in hand gazing at one another. Alyson could feel the warmth of closeness spread through her and thought again how nice this felt and how she could get use to looking at this face, this man.

Kathy's excited voice reminded them that they were not alone.

"I know, I know! I remember now where I've seen her!"

"You've seen who?" Alyson found herself asking Kathy.

"Calm down Kathy. Why don't you come over here and sit down? Now let's start over slowly," Darrell instructed after Kathy was seated between the two of them.

"Daddy says that when I get excited I talk a mile a minute and he can't understand a word I'm saying, so he makes me sit down and count to five slowly then say what ever it is I need to say," Kathy explained to Alyson.

"Now Kathy what were you trying to say before?" Darrell asked patiently.

"Daddy when I first looked at the lady in the picture, she pointed to the picture on the sofa table, she looked like someone I'd seen before, but I couldn't remember where. Now I remember." Kathy finished quite pleased with her discovery.

"Kathy are you sure It's the lady in this picture that you saw?" Darrell asked not looking at his daughter but at Alyson who was not saying anything, but looked as if the wind had been knocked out of her.

"Of course I'm sure Daddy."

"Where? When?" Alyson was unable to say anything more.

"At our girl scout meeting," Kathy looked at Alyson.

"What do you mean?" Darrell asked.

"Well not exactly *at* our meeting. Daddy you know you drop me off at Felicity's house every other Saturday at ten o'clock. Felicity is my best friend," Kathy turned to Alyson to explain. "Her mom takes us to our girl scout meeting at Morning Star Baptist Church. Well for the last two meetings we've had we had to go and help out at the mission there. *That's* where I saw her. She was there."

"Kathy, are you sure?" Darrell asked his daughter again not knowing whether or not she understood the importance of what she was saying.

Alyson found her voice again and reached out and put her arms around Kathy's shoulders turning the little girl to face her. "Kathy my sister has been missing for more than a year now. Are you sure that you saw the lady in this picture?"

"Yes ma'am," Kathy said slowly, "but I didn't know she was your sister. If you don't believe me you can go with me to our meeting tomorrow."

Alyson could see something akin to hope in the little girl's eyes.

"I think that we will all be going to the meeting tomorrow," Darrell said.

"Alyson you're not angry with me are you?"

Alyson looked at the little girl whose face was turned to hers and said, "No sweetie, of course I'm not angry. I'm really very happy about what you've just told me."

"Then why are you crying? I didn't mean to make you cry," Kathy said earnestly.

"Honey, I'm okay, truly I am and I'm not angry," Alyson said as she brushed away the trace of tears from her eyes.

"Promise?"

"I promise. Girl Scouts honor," Alyson said and smiled.

"You were a girl scout too?" Kathy asked excitedly.

"Yes, many years ago."

"Wow." Kathy said with pure admiration in her eyes.

"To prove to you that I'm okay why don't you go in the kitchen and get us all some ice cream. I have fudge and pecans on the counter near the fridge."

"I love ice cream!" Kathy said as she jumped off the sofa and practically ran to the refrigerator.

"The bowls are in the dishwasher," she said to Kathy's retreating frame.

"Alyson are you sure you're okay?" Darrell asked when he was sure that his daughter was busy with her task and out of hearing range.

She could see the concern in his eyes. "I think so." She said as she picked up the picture of her sister. "I'm afraid to even think of the possibility," she said quietly. "What if it really is Alicia?"

He took her hands in his and said, "We'll find out for sure tomorrow."

"Darrell should I call the police?"

"No, not yet. Let's wait until we know for certain. I'm not sure how you're going to feel about this, but I'd like to pray with you if you don't mind."

Alyson gently pulled her hands from him and walked over to the double glass doors that led to her balcony. She stared past her own reflection into the night, thoughts racing through her head, emotions tearing at her heart. He wanted to pray. All of a sudden she felt so timid. She had to explain to him that she didn't share his beliefs. She didn't want to offend him. She didn't want him to think badly of her. She had to choose her words carefully for she really did want to see him again after tonight, after tomorrow morning.

"Darrell I know that you are a religious man, but," she hesitated briefly then took the plunge, "I don't share those beliefs. I'm not saying that I don't believe there's a God or some higher power, or something, but not to the extent in which you do. I mean religion just doesn't fit into the scheme of things in my life. I know that's probably disappointing to you. I know it is to my mother." Alyson laughed nervously. "That's why I never took you up on you offer to go to church. My mother says she keeps me in her prayers and she knows one day I'll come around, but I don't see that happening." Alyson looked intently at the reflection of the face that had joined hers in the glass of the door. Hands on her shoulder gently turned her to face him. Alyson kept her focus on the buttons of his shirt. She was afraid to look into his eyes. She was afraid of what she might see.

"I know that you must be feeling a lot of different emotions right now. I'm not here to sit in judgment about what you believe. Alyson," he said her name softly as he put his hand under her chin to lift her head so that her eyes could meet his. "I just want to pray that you find peace especially tonight and that there is calm for your fears and that you will be able to rest comfortably and that tomorrow will bring resolution to your pain and the restitution of your joy."

He took her hands in his and he prayed.

After he said 'Amen,' Alyson lifted her eyes to his. He was still holding both her hands. He lifted them and kissed first the one and then the other all the while looking deeply into her eyes. "I know that this may not be the right time to say this, but I like you very much." With a feather light touch, he brushed her bangs aside and placed a single kiss on her forehead.

Alyson looked into his eyes and she saw in their depths a reinforcement of his admission. At that moment she felt what no man had ever made her feel. Shyness. Not even as an adolescent had she ever felt this way for she was always in control. "I like you too." She smiled up at him, surprising herself.

"There are a lot of hours between now and tomorrow morning. If you need someone to talk to, no matter how late you think it is I want you to call me. Okay?"

She was about to object, but the look in his eyes told her he wouldn't hear of it so she simply said, "Okay."

"We should probably get going. I'm sure you probably need some time alone. Though I must admit I'm reluctant to leave you after laying this bomb on you."

"It's okay. I do need some time to sort out my thoughts and feelings." Alyson saw Kathy come back into the room. "I thought you were getting us ice cream," she said to Kathy trying to sound cheerful for the little girl's benefit.

"I ate mine in the kitchen so you guys could talk grown-up without a little kid hanging around." Kathy grinned at them both.

"You know for a little kid, you're pretty grown-up," Alyson said as she hugged Kathy not at all surprised by her actions.

"I want to thank you for a wonderful evening," Darrell said.

"Yeah, it was really cool!" Kathy chimed in.

He put his hand to her cheek. "Goodnight Alyson. Remember what I said. If you need to talk, call me. I'll pick you up at nine a.m." He said goodnight again and he and Kathy left.

Alone with her thoughts, Alyson resolved not to think about anything until she had made herself a cup of tea. That done, she sat on the sofa with her sister's picture on her lap, questions racing through her mind.

The person that Kathy was sure she had seen was probably not her sister. How could she be? But if she were her sister, then why hadn't she contacted them? It didn't make any sense. With no answers to her questions, Alyson got ready for bed even though she knew that she would get very little sleep tonight if any at all. Several times she picked up the phone to call Darrell and decided against it. She had never been dependent on any man before and she certainly wasn't going to start now!

Alyson turned over and looked again at the clock for the one-thousandth time. Only 3:00 a.m. If she didn't do something, anything she was going to go out of her mind with all the congestion of things running through it! Without her usual contemplation of things and before she lost her nerve, she got up, dressed and was in her car and on the interstate before rational thought took hold. "I must be losing my mind!" Alyson said to herself. Calling him at 3 a.m. was one thing, but showing up on his doorstep at 3 a.m. was entirely another matter! What was he going to think of her? "I tell you what he's going to think. Insane! He's going to think that I've taken leave of my senses!" She spoke aloud to the rear lights of the car some distance in front of her, but she forged ahead.

Earlier in the week out of curiosity she had plugged his address in the map program on her computer and it had printed out a nice little route from her door to his, not that she had ever planned to use it. But here she was following it to the letter. Turning into the subdivision she noted the houses, though it was too dark to see much detail. They seemed large with sprawling lawns unlike a lot of subdivisions she saw going up with small homes that were so close to the other person you could practically have breakfast together! She soon found the house bearing the right address and pulled slowly into the driveway. Immediately a light came on and flooded the inside of her car, making her feel like a criminal caught in the spot light. Realizing that it was just a motion detection light, she found her way easily to the front door via the lighted path.

She could hear the doorbell resounding through the house. The door itself was a magnificent array of crystal and wood with small panes framing the sides and a half moon on the top. A light came on somewhere in the interior of the house that softly lit the foyer within. A barefooted Darrell in a deep blue robe opened the door.

"Alyson? Is everything okay? Come on in."

She could tell that he was confused and surprised to see her as she stepped into the foyer of his home. "I know you must be surprised to see me. I'm sorry to just show up at your house like this." Alyson said feeling more than a little embarrassed by her actions.

"No problem. I was hoping that if you needed someone tonight. I mean to talk to that you would turn to me."

The rich timber of his voice instantly put her at ease. "I tried to sleep but my mind kept racing so I got up, but the walls just seem to be closing in on me and I well...Here I am," she finished somewhat sheepishly.

"It's okay. In all honestly I wasn't getting much sleep either. I didn't know just how what my daughter had said was affecting you. I picked up the phone any number of times to call you, but I didn't want to crowd you or anything."

Alyson found his concern touching. "I was going to call *you* but I didn't quite know what to say."

"I could get us some coffee if you'd like?" He inquired as he showed her into an interior room of the house.

"That would be nice."

While he was gone, Alyson took the opportunity to survey her surroundings. It was a large room with two overstuffed sofas in an L-shape position with two matching chairs opposite them and a large coffee table between them. The floors were hardwood with a large oriental rug covering the sitting area. A huge television with speakers just as large was the focal point of the room. There were built in bookcases on either side of the fireplace as well as on two other walls. Alyson stopped at the mantel of the fireplace, which bore an assortment of family pictures. One was of an attractive woman and Kathy. The two had the same smile and dimpled cheeks.

"Kathy and Melissa took that picture just before we found out about the cancer." Darrell said as he came back into the room bearing a tray.

Alyson noticed that he had also changed into a shirt and slacks, but was still barefoot.

"She's very pretty."

"Yes."

"Kathy must miss her mother a lot."

"Yes she does. As a father, I try but sometimes a girl just needs a mother. Melissa was an only child herself. My sister tries to help out as much as she can, but she's pretty busy with her own family now that there's a new baby. My mom has been great though. I don't know what I would do without her."

They were now seated on one of the large comfortable sofas, steaming cups of coffee in hand.

"I want to thank you for being so kind as to allow me into your home after showing up here the way I've done."

"Knight Darrell Henderson at you service ma'am," he said as he smiled at her.

She didn't feel pressured to talk. The conversation seemed to flow of its own volition. She talked about growing up with her sister, grade school, middle school, and high school. By the time she got through the college years, she had slipped off her shoes, tucked her feet under her on the sofa, and was cuddled underneath a large chenille afghan that Darrell had given her. He listened intently to her every word, laughing at the funny parts and concerned at the sad parts.

"The rest of the story you've heard." Alyson said when she got to the part where Alicia had not made it to their lunch date. "For so long I've had no answers to my questions and right now I'm just afraid to hope. I'm afraid of what it means if it really is my sister that Kathy saw and yet I'm afraid to get my hopes up only to find out it's not really her. I guess that sounds silly."

"Not at all. I can't imagine what this past year has been like for you."

It struck her again how nice this man was and how different he was from any other she had known. She felt totally at ease even on his turf.

"Alyson I know that we don't share the same beliefs and mind you I am in no way trying to force mine on you, but I would like to pray with you again. If it's okay with you?"

Alyson didn't quite know what to say. He was asking yet again to pray with her. She didn't know what good would come of it. He was looking at her expecting an answer and it came forth on a single breath before she had time to think of a way out. "Yes."

He took her hands in his. "I will kneel here beside the sofa but you don't have to." He said as he did so.

Out of awkwardness, Alyson followed his lead and knelt beside him and as he bowed his head so did she.

He began to pray.

Oh heavenly Father, I first acknowledge Your sovereignty. I bow before You in total submission unto You. I praise Your name for You and You alone are worthy to be praised. I lift You up before all men for You said if I would do so that You would draw all men unto You. Father one of your beloved is lost from among us. We know that You know all things and that all things are in Your control. I don't know what tomorrow will bring or even what the next moment will bring but Lord I trust in You and I know that You have worked all things for our good and Your perfect plan. I pray that Your will be done and that You give your daughter Alyson the understanding that she desires and the peace that she seeks so desperately. Lord, answer her cries as she stands at Your threshold. Wrap Your loving arms around her so that she will know that You love unconditionally and that her heart, her life is safe with You. I Love You Father. I pray this in Your loving son Jesus' name and we submit ourselves as You guide us into all truth and understanding. Amen. Amen. Amen.

Alyson could hear the Amen but could not respond. The tears were slipping past even though she squeezed her eyelids tightly. She could feel arms around her as Darrell pulled her to him. And she cried. Cried for her sister and cried for herself.

When the storm inside had calmed, she pulled away shyly. "I'm sorry." She couldn't look at him.
"No need to apologize."

She still felt the need to somehow explain for raining all over the guy the way she had done. "It's just that, well I probably haven't prayed since my mother use to make us pray as children. I mean it was very touching what you said. I know that you've never met her, but while you were praying it was as if you actually cared about her. I know that sounds silly."

He put his hands to her cheeks and brushed away a falling tear with his thumb. "I care about you Alyson Edwards and anything and anyone that affects you. I know it's crazy, we've just met and yet ...I can't explain it."

Alyson looked into his eyes and she could see the sincerity in which he spoke. When his lips touched hers tentative at first she responded in kind. The kiss deepened as the response in her did. He pulled away and placed a kiss on her forehead and on each cheek. Before she could stop them the words rushed forth from her heart. "I care about you too Darrell Henderson," surprising her own ears.

He took her hands in his and kissed the palm of each.

A surge of electricity went through her giving light to all the dark places.

He settled her on the sofa and tucked the chenille afghan around her. "I'll be right back," he said as he headed toward the kitchen. He returned shortly with a cup and saucer.

The warm liquid felt good although she didn't recognize the flavor. She looked up at him a silent question in her eyes.

"It's chamomile tea. It's reported to have a soothing effect."

She took another sip. "It's good. I like it! Thank you Darrell. I wasn't sure how I was going to get through this night."

"My pleasure," he said.

They talked for some time afterwards. He shared his own childhood days and she couldn't help but laugh at some of the 'adventures' he and his siblings created.

Chapter 6

"Dad?"

She could hear the small voice but couldn't seem to pull her eyes open. There it goes again, she heard it once more. Only when she heard her own name and remembered where she was did she reach full consciousness. She must have fallen asleep. She was sitting on the sofa beside Darrell, her head on his chest, his arm around her. Though they were both fully clothed, when she looked up into Kathy's small face she blushed and to make matters worse, Darrell was awake now too! She avoided eye contact with either him or his daughter as she began extricating herself from the sofa.

"Hi Alyson, when did you get here? Are you staying for breakfast? Dad makes the best waffles. Wait until you taste them! Dad you will make us waffles, won't you?"

Alyson was thankful for Kathy's chatter for she needed a moment to compose herself. Thank goodness for the innocence of a child, she thought.

"Of course, I'll make breakfast and waffles it is. Alyson, Kathy can show you were the guest bedroom is, there's a bath and you can freshen up there if you like."

Only then did she make eye contact with him. "Thank you, I'd like that." Alyson took Kathy's hand. "Lead the way," she said to her little guide.

"After breakfast I'll give you the grand tour. I can't wait for you to see my room. It's the coolest. Oh Alyson I'm so glad you're here!" Kathy hugged her excitedly and talked all the way to the guest room, which was located down the hall from the foyer on the front side of the house.

The guest room was fabulous, decorated in blue and lavender with accents of deep purple. The adjourning bathroom was more of the same with gleaming gold faucets and marble tile. There was a large garden tub surrounded by candles in crystal holders. There was a separate frosted glass encased shower. True to his word it was equipped with anything she might need. After a hot shower, she applied sparse make-up and combed through her hair. She had been trying not to think about the predicament she had found herself in earlier. How was she going to face him? Though it was innocent enough, her cheeks grew warm with the embarrassment of it.

She remembered having the dream again and seeing her sister's reflection in the water instead of her own. She must have been crying in her sleep because she remembered arms enfolding her in warmth and she remembered a strong timbered voice calling her name and saying everything would be okay. It'll be all right over and over again. Alyson marveled at how safe she felt with this man. "Careful girl, this could be addictive," she admonished herself. She tidied up the bathroom and went in search of the wonderful aroma that was undoubtedly coming from the kitchen.

Alyson found her way back to the family room and from it she could observe the man in the kitchen. He had changed into a navy print shirt and jeans and he was singing. He really was quite a handsome man and his singing voice was actually quite good. Alyson did a quick assessment; a man who can navigate a kitchen, sing and was easy on the eyes too. Now that was more than any girl could hope for! "Easy girl," she admonished herself for the second time. Well she had to face him sooner or later.

"Hey is there anything I can do to help?" She avoided eye contact and picked up an oven mitt that lay on the countertop.

"No, everything's under control and just about ready."

"Where's Kathy?"

"She's in the garage making sure all the things we need to take down to the mission are boxed and ready to go."

His mention of the mission reminded her of the thing that she had been avoiding more than eye contact with Darrell. The mission. Her sister. Darrell was standing in front of her now.

"Alyson are you okay?" He took the oven mitt from her so that he could hold her hands.

"Yeah, sure," she said aware that she didn't even sound convincing to herself.

"You were crying in your sleep and I tried to wake you but you didn't respond. You kept crying so I just held you. I just wanted to comfort you. That's all. I'm sorry I didn't mean to cause you any embarrassment."

"You don't have to apologize," she said looking into his eyes. "Thank you for being there with me, for allowing me to camp out on your doorstep, and for sticking by me through all this. I don't know what the outcome will be but I am grateful that you're here and that I don't have to go through this alone."

"Do you want to talk about it?"

"Yes. No," she corrected herself. "Maybe later." She had not yet told him about the dream.

"I won't press you, but know that if you need to talk, I'm here."

"Thanks Darrell."

"Hey it sure smells good in here. Is it time to eat?" Kathy burst through a side door into the kitchen.

"Yes it is. Why don't you two get the plates from the cabinet and the juice from the refrigerator while I finish up these eggs?"

"Didn't I tell you Dad makes the best waffles?" Kathy said to Alyson.

"Yes you did!" Alyson said finishing off the last of the juice in her glass. When she had first come into the kitchen she didn't think she would be able to sit at a table let alone eat a meal, but looking at her clean plate now, she was feeling pleasurably full. Waffles with real maple syrup, eggs prepared with fresh bell pepper, onions, mushrooms and just a touch of parmesan cheese and fresh cantaloupe slices. "It was wonderful! My compliments to the chef." Alyson said looking over at Darrell.

"Compliment accepted," he said to Alyson then looking at his daughter inquired, "Is everything all set in the garage?"

"Yes Dad. It's ready to go."

"I'll load the dishwasher and then we'll be ready to go."

"I can do that." Alyson volunteered.

"No ma'am, you are a guest in our home and you will do no such thing, but there is something you can do," he said to her.

"Anything." Alyson said earnestly wanting to keep her mind on the moment and not on the one to come.

"You can pull the truck out of the garage," he said as he tossed her the keys.

The 'truck' was a dark blue Ford Expedition fully loaded and immaculate inside and out. Alyson noticed that there was also a black BMW parked beside it. After pushing the garage door opener she inched the truck out of the garage. It's a good thing she had parked on the side of the driveway closest to the house, she noted as she came to a stop beside her own car. Today! How was she going to get through today? One moment at a time, that's how. She couldn't, wouldn't let herself think of the appointed hour to come. The sound of voices pulled her thoughts back to the moment and she watched as Darrell with Kathy in tow opened the back hatch of the truck and began loading boxes, which were labeled either clothes or goods.

The loading of the boxes took only a few minutes and then they were on their way. No one spoke. It was as if they had formed an unspoken pack of silence. They were soon on the interstate and still no one spoke. Solitude cloaked Alyson and weighed heavily on her shoulders. She didn't realize that her hands were tightly clenched in her lap until Darrell reached over and covered them with his own. He didn't speak. He just held them.

They soon pulled into the parking lot of a fairly large building bearing the name 'Morning Star Mission.'

"Daddy is it okay if I go join Karen and her Mom, they just pulled up too?" Kathy said breaking the silence.

"Sure you go on, we'll be right behind you in a moment."

Alyson sat rigid looking straight ahead intent on the sign above the door of the mission afraid to focus on anything that lay beyond. Darrell had come around and opened her door but she still couldn't move. She couldn't make her legs step outside of the truck. It was as if her legs were solidly apart of the very interior of the vehicle.

"Alyson I will be with you, beside you. I will not leave you."

She heard his voice. She could feel his hands as they closed around hers, their warmth melting the bands of apprehension that held her captive. "Have you ever had the feeling that your life was about to be changed forever?" Alyson spoke in a voice that sounded foreign to her own ears. "That no matter what you did or didn't do your life was on some sort of unalterable course," Alyson continued speaking her eyes never wavering from the sign above the door of the building in front of her.

Darrell placed his hands one on either side of her face gently forcing her eyes to look into his own. "Often. I get that feeling often and I embrace it because I know that my life is in God's hands. I'm grateful for it has brought many wonderful things into my life and now it has brought me you." He smiled.

Alyson smiled with wonder in return and allowed him to help her out of the truck.

The mission was full. There were people everywhere coming and going. There were people being fed, there were people receiving clothing goods, there was a place for people to sleep that had no place to go. All around her there were people who needed help and people giving help. Alyson had convinced Darrell that she needed to go in alone and respecting her wishes he had honored her request with the assurance that he would be close by should she need him. Looking around her she saw no one who resembled her sister. There was a lady making a bed nearby which was in a row of many.

"Excuse me ma'am, I was wondering if you've seen anyone here who looks like the lady in this picture? She's my sister," Alyson explained in response to the questioning look on the stranger's face before her.

The lady looked at the picture. "I do believe so. She's helping out in the kitchen today. The kitchens right through those doors." The lady said pointing to the doors not too many feet away.

"Thank you," Alyson said and willed her legs to close the distance between her and the doors that led to the kitchen and... She couldn't even finish the thought. She hesitated only a moment then pushed the heavy doors gaining access to a whole different world of sights and smells. There were ladies stirring huge pots on a large stove and others doing various other chores. Alyson scanned the room, her eyes missing nothing and noting each face none of which looked like her sister.

"Excuse me, can I help you?" A voice spoke from behind.

Startled, Alyson dropped the picture she was holding. She could feel the hair stand up on the back of her neck and it seemed as if the world shifted into slow motion. She bent down to pick up the picture and rose. Then she turned and at that same instance her eyes collided with familiar brown eyes and then a face as familiar as her own.

They stood face-to-face and eye-to-eye.

"Are you okay?" The face asked.

The words even seem to come in slow motion. Alyson felt as if someone had knocked the wind from her lungs.

"Alicia!" The single word burst forth on a single strangled breath.

Caught Up

L.A.Fowlkes

THE REVELATION

Caught Up

Chapter 7

"I'll get you a glass of water. Sit down here." The voice was leading her through the kitchen outside to a bench beside the door.

Reaching to take the glass her hand shook noticeably. The cool liquid felt soothing somehow and slowly the world around her returned to a normal pace.

"Are you going to be all right?" The voice asked again.

Alyson turned to face the voice. Familiar eyes. Familiar face. "Alicia I can't believe it! You're alive!" She grabbed and hugged the owner of the voice, the tears blurring her vision. "We thought you were dead. I can't believe it!" When she pulled back from the embrace, the eyes of the voice were not joyous as she herself was, but puzzled.

"Why do you call me Alicia?" She said.

"Because you are," was all that Alyson could think to say.

"My name is Beth. Beth Avery."

Alyson looked at her disbelieving. Her name wasn't Beth. It was Alicia.

During the earlier days of her sister's disappearance when she had refused to believe that her sister was lying dead somewhere she never thought for one moment that Alicia might be somewhere for whatever reason suffering from amnesia! But it must be so for the woman before her was surely her sister. How in the world was she going to handle this *new* development? Amnesia?

"You dropped what looked to be a photograph. May I see it?" The woman who called herself Beth asked.

"Yes, sure. It's my sister." Alyson said as her voice faltered slightly and she handed the picture to the woman who called herself Beth. She watched as she studied the picture. There was no sign of recognition on her face, nor in her eyes.

"She's very pretty."

"You look so much like her."

"Yes, I can see why you might think so."

Alyson took a moment to study the woman beside her. Same shade of brown hair as her sister's, though this woman had hers pulled back on either side with hair clips, same build, same facial features. Caught in the act, Alyson couldn't look away as their eyes met again, same familiar eyes and yet they seemed not quite so. The eyes are the mirror of the soul, the thought seem to come from nowhere. Her eyes *were* the same and yet *not* the same. "You look so much like her." Alyson found herself saying again still clinging to her earlier explanation that this was indeed her sister, her sister with amnesia.

"I assure you that I am not her."

"But how do you know you're not her?" Alyson knew that her question was a shot in the dark but she asked it anyway. In answer to the puzzled look from the familiar eyes, Alyson tried to explain. "I mean what if you are her and something happened and you just can't remember?"

"Because I know who I am and where I come from."

"How do you know? How do you *really* know for sure?" Alyson said persistently.

"Because I know who I am and where I come from." The woman who called herself Beth was just as persistent.

"If you're not my sister then who are you and where have you come from?" Alyson turned the reply into a question of her own.

"If you'd like to talk, I'll be done here at two o'clock. I could meet you some place." The familiar face said patiently.

"I'd like that. Why don't I pick you up here if that's okay with you?"

"That'll be fine."

Alyson and the woman with the familiar eyes who's name was Beth, Beth Avery rose simultaneously.

"Good then. I'm sorry. In all the confusion I forgot to introduce myself. My name is Alyson Edwards," she said feeling somewhat awkward as she extended her hand. There wasn't even a flicker of recognition from the familiar face.

"Pleased to meet you Ms. Edwards." The familiar face grasped and shook her extended hand.

Something unexplainable seemed to grip Alyson in the instant Beth's hand gripped her own. It wasn't something unpleasant, but quite the contrary. It was soothing and peaceful. How very odd Alyson thought to herself not sure what to make of what had transpired at the moment of contact. "I'll see you at two then."

"Yes at two."

The women parted company and the woman with the familiar face and the familiar eyes named Beth, Beth Avery, went back to her work and Alyson went in search of Darrell and Kathy.

Mission accomplished, she found Darrell in the parking lot of the mission. The Girl Scout troop had already left and Kathy had gone home with her friend Felicity.

"What happened to you? One moment you where there and the next you were gone?" Darrell asked the moment he saw her approaching. "Did you find her?"

"Yes. She was in the kitchen. Darrell she didn't even recognize me." Alyson said as she looked into his eyes, now familiar eyes, comforting eyes. "She said that her name is Beth. Beth Avery." She felt arms pull her close as he hugged her. "Oh Darrell what am I going to do now? It's Alicia! I know it is and yet..." She paused looking for the right words to finish.

"Yet what?"

"It's like she's not herself somehow. I can't explain it. She's agreed to meet with me to talk." Alyson said as she pulled back from his embrace, immediately missing the warmth. "I'm picking her up here at two o'clock."

"I'm here if you need me to tag along." He offered.

"I think maybe I need to speak with her alone. But thank you. You've been great."

"Then I'll take you back to the house so you can get your car."

Both remained silent during the drive back to the house. No one spoke until they pulled up into the driveway.

"Darrell what if she has amnesia and just can't remember who she is?" Alyson broke the silence.

"Are you sure that this woman *is* you sister?"

"Yes of course I'm sure. Darrell I'm going to be up front with you. There was a moment when I looked into her eyes that I knew she was Alicia and yet she wasn't Alicia. I know that sounds a little crazy but I can't explain it and then when I shook her hand I felt this strange calm, peaceful feeling." Totally at a loss Alyson sat, silent again.

"Will you call me later?" It was Darrell who broke the silence this time.

"Yes I will. Thank you. I don't know how I could have made it through last night let alone this morning without you." She meant it with everything in her.

"My pleasure," he said as he leaned over and kissed her.

She was growing to like this man and the way he cared for her.

It was one o'clock when she returned to the mission. One hour to wait. Alyson decided to use the time to plan her strategy. How was she going to get her sister to remember who she was? Should she call the police now or wait? Should she tell her parents that Alicia was here alive or wait? All were questions in which she had no answers. Through all the uncertainty she knew that somehow she would have to get Alicia to trust her first. Alyson sat in her car intently watchful of the mission's front door. Just as they had agreed, the woman who called herself Beth, Beth Avery emerged through the opened door promptly at two o'clock and seeing Alyson in the waiting car, walked up to the driver's side.

"I've been working in the mission all morning. If it's okay with you, I'd like to go home and freshen up a bit." The woman spoke.

"Sure, I'll drive you home." Alyson said to the familiar face with the familiar voice.

"It's not that far from here. Thank you, I really appreciate it."

The place where she was staying was a couple of blocks from the mission, Alyson soon discovered. The house was a large colonial style that had been renovated into separate apartments.

"You can come in if you'd like instead of waiting out here."

"Thank you." Alyson said, her curiosity getting the best of her. Odd that she didn't feel fearful or even mistrustful. Goodness knows one had only to see a small segment of the daily news to hear of the many atrocities that went on in any large city, and Atlanta was no exception.

The apartment this woman occupied was sparsely furnished and with her in the other room, Alyson took a moment to take in every detail of her surroundings. The room was simply furnished with a small sofa and chair. There were no pictures of any kind on the walls in fact there wasn't even one visible photograph anywhere that she could see.

If her sister thought herself to be Beth Avery so be it, Alyson decided. She would call her that until she could learn more about what had happened and where her sister had been for a whole year. Beth emerged from the other room dressed casually in a yellow sleeveless sundress and sandals.

"Where would you like to go to talk?" She asked.

Alyson had been wondering about that very same thing when it came to her. It was a brilliant idea! "I have a place in mind. It shouldn't be too crowded now that lunch is over and it's still a little early for the dinner crowd."

They drove along silently to the café. Alyson had decided on the little café across from the hospital where she and her sister often met for lunch and where they would have, had things turned out differently, a year ago. She hoped that it might trigger some sort of memories for this familiar stranger beside her.

The lunch crowd had thinned out just as she had anticipated. It was a beautiful day and they were able to get a table outside under the eaves. The waiter brought them tall glasses of iced tea and still neither woman broke the silence between them. Alyson observed intently the woman across from her, and yet she seemed not to show any sign that she remembered ever being in this place.

"It's nice here," the familiar stranger said.

Alyson silently screamed, "Alicia don't you remember we come here often?" The familiar stranger acted as if none of this was familiar to her. She seemed not to even recognize a sister that she had shared a womb with and a lifetime with.

"May I see the picture you have of her again?"

Alyson pulled the picture from her purse and handed it to the familiar stranger who called herself Beth.

"Was she happy here?" The woman asked still looking at the photograph.

Alyson tried to remember when the picture was taken. It was the Christmas before her disappearance. "Yes she was happy. Christmas seems to have that affect on my family as well as a lot of other families."

"I'm sorry, I *meant* was her life a joyous one?" The woman named Beth tried to clarify her earlier statement and this time looked intently at Alyson.

"Well yes. I suppose she was happy." Alyson thought how strange the question sounded and even stranger that she should be answering it considering the person who they where talking about sat right across from her and had been the one asking the question!

"Tell me about her."

Alyson and Beth talked well into the evening. When the sun began its decent they moved inside and had dinner still talking although Alyson did most of the talking prompted by simple questions from Beth.

Alyson returned to her apartment after dropping Beth at hers. After checking her messages and getting herself a cup of tea, she sat down to think about the afternoon and evening. How is it she had gone to question Beth, but she had done most of the talking, answering questions, giving information all evening long?

She remembered the question that had prompted the conversation. Beth had asked if Alicia had been happy. Alyson thought about that now. In truth she wasn't really sure. Thinking back she knew that her sister took to heart the injustices of the world against women and especially the children. She knew that her sister had been saddened by the fact that so many children slipped through the cracks of society and the system put in place for their welfare and that she considered it her personal mission to help remedy the problems. In a world that seemed to care little if its little ones were left unloved and unwanted, her sister had given countless hours helping at shelters and orphanages. She was in a mentoring program and in Big Brothers and Sisters. The list of her involvements was numerous beginning from early adolescent. Now thinking back to the earlier question she wasn't so sure if her sister was happy. Only Alicia herself could answer that one. She *could* say for certain that Alicia was happiest when she was helping others.

Alyson had promised to call Darrell and she dialed his number. "Hi Darrell, it's Alyson. I called to give you an update on my meeting with uh Beth." It was still hard for her to call her sister Beth.

"So how'd it go?" He asked in that deep voice Alyson couldn't seem to get enough of hearing.

"I'm not so sure, since I did most of the talking!" Alyson grimaced to herself.

"Are you still convinced that she's your sister?"

"Well, she certainly looks and sounds like her but she seems different. There's something about her that is not usual. I don't know. I can't seem to put my finger on it."

"Does she make you uncomfortable in any way?"

"No it's nothing like that, in fact when I'm around her I feel just the opposite." Alyson said unable to clear up her own confusion let alone try to make things clear for him. She told him again about what she had experienced earlier when she had shaken Beth's hand. "Darrell it was the weirdest thing. I felt such a peace. I can't put it into words and I'm usually never at a loss for words, but I am here."

"So what's next?"

"Well since my attempt to draw her out failed today, I guess I'll be meeting with her until I get to the truth." Alyson said speculatively.

"Are you planning to notify the authorities?"

"I don't think so, at least not yet."

"And what about your parents?"

"I don't want to risk it yet, not until I can get some answers. Darrell there's something else. She invited me to church, *her* church tomorrow. She says she's singing and would like it if I came."

"What's the matter?"

Alyson could hear the concern in his voice. "Well I'm sure it's nothing but Alicia had, *has*," she corrected herself, "a beautiful singing voice. The service is at eleven a.m. If you and Kathy could come with me I would be eternally in your debt. I know that you have your own church service to go to but I would appreciate it very much."

"Say no more. How about we pick you up about ten fifteen in the morning?"

"That would be great. Thank you Darrell."

"You are most welcome."

There was a pause on both ends of the phone line then Darrell spoke. "I have a confession to make." His voice lowered and sounded as if he were right beside her.

"And what might that be?" Alyson said a little breathlessly.

"I was hoping that you would have stopped by tonight after your meeting, but just the same I'm glad you called."

"I thought of doing just that but decided I didn't want to push my luck after dropping by unexpectedly *and* unannounced last night." Alyson laughed into the phone.

"No matter how last night came about, I'm glad you feel as if you can confide in me."

"I'm glad too." Alyson found herself saying in truth. "I'll see you in the morning."

"Goodnight."

The next morning, Alyson dressed in a slim tan dress suit with matching pumps and just the right touch of make-up, answered the knock on her door. She knew it was Darrell so she grabbed her purse and keys.

"You look great!" He said and kissed her cheek.

"Thanks. Where's Kathy?" Alyson said to cover up the blush his compliment had evoked.

"She's waiting in the car."

"Okay let's do this." She said as she locked her apartment door behind them and linked her arm through the one Darrell offered. Today they were in the BMW sedan. Alyson took in the feel of the leather beneath her. "Nice car."

"Yeah I guess so. I'd rather drive the truck, but Kathy insists that we drive the car on Sundays to church. She thinks it's more civilized." He smiled in the rear view mirror.

"Oh Dad!" Kathy responded, both father and daughter shared a smile.

"You look very pretty today." Alyson spoke to Kathy.

"Thank you. I think it's great that you're inviting us to go to church. I like our church, but sometimes it's nice to go visit other places. It's like an adventure!"

Alyson had no idea how prophetic those words would become. The church was located close to the mission and its parking lot was already filling to capacity as well as the pews inside. The usher seated them near the rear of the church since that was the only place where the three of them could sit together. She and Kathy sat on either side of Darrell. The service had not yet begun but the musicians were playing softly. Alyson took the time to acquaint herself with her surroundings. The building itself was just large enough for a nice crowd. There were people of varying ages, young mothers with babies, fathers and sons, grandparents and grandchildren.

It had been some time since she had stepped foot inside a church. How odd though that it felt as if it were just yesterday and she and Alicia were children getting ready for Sunday service. Alicia would often sing solo or the lead in songs, her voice a beautiful sound filling the church. Her

mother would often say that God had given Alicia
the voice of an angel. Alyson agreed for there was
something about hearing Alicia sing that moved
one beyond that which was emotional. As they
had grown from children to young adults then to
women, so too had Alicia's voice matured,
strengthening in character, depth, and range.
Though Alyson no longer attended church not
even to hear her sister sing, she often enjoyed
her sister's voice as she sang at family gatherings,
joined by her father who leant the perfect blend
of his baritone to produce a sound that went
unmatched even in today's array of musical talent.

The music picked up and stirred her from her
sojourn into the past. The choir took its place and
a group consisting of seven women and men led
the congregation into a moving rendition of first
upbeat then slow moving songs of praise and
worship. Much to her surprise, Alyson found
herself enjoying it. She enjoyed hearing Darrell's
deep voice beside her as she caught on easily to
the repetitive words of the songs.

After the praise and worship, the congregation
was lead in prayer and all were instructed to hold
the hand of the person on either side. Alyson felt
Darrell enclose her right hand and a woman her
left. She tried to focus on the words surrounding
her and the strength and solid assurance in which
Darrell held her own hand. When the prayer was
finished and they had taken their seats, Darrell
continued to hold her hand. Alyson had noticed
the families around her and as she looked at the
hand that held hers now she felt a similar bond.
She had never thought much about having a

family of her own in recent years, but this felt good. It really felt good.

The choir sang a song and people clapped their hands in time to the rhythm and others who knew the words joined in and sang along. Alyson had seen Alicia or Beth as she wanted to be called, come in with the choir. She was seated in the third row.

As the music began for the second song, Beth moved apart from the group to a waiting microphone. The music was slow and stirring then Beth began to sing and the voice that came forth filled the building. Alyson closed her eyes and the voice surrounded her and she was transported into a time when Alicia sang with the voice of an angel and she with open arms reached out to it welcoming her sister home. Alyson knew that tears were falling, but she didn't care. The tears were tears of joy for this woman had to be Alicia for *no* two people could sing so much alike in all the world!

After the service they waited in front of the church knowing that Beth would find them.

"Darrell it's her! I know it's her! When she was singing it was as if the heavens opened up!" Alyson exclaimed as she closed her eyes and remembered the moment, feeling excited and somewhat fearful.

"If you're convinced that she's your sister, what now?"

"I don't know." Alyson lowered her voice as Beth approached. She introduced Beth to Darrell and Kathy being careful to call her sister Beth and not Alicia.

"It's a pleasure to meet you Beth. I must say that you have a beautiful voice." Darrell greeted the stranger.

"Yes absolutely incredible!" Alyson joined the compliment.

"Thank you both. I really love to sing." Beth said.

Alyson could see the apparent pleasure in her eyes, familiar eyes that seemed to radiate forth and surround her very presence. Alyson mentally shook herself. It must be the sunlight shining into her eyes. Alyson looked down at her shoes momentarily to shield her eyes.

"Why don't you join us for dinner?" Darrell asked Beth.

"I really don't want to intrude on your family plans," Beth responded.

At the mention of them being a family with family plans, Alyson looked up. "It's really no bother. We would like it very much if you would join us." She hadn't known that they had had plans for dinner until now. It would be interesting to know Darrell's opinion of Beth and perhaps she might learn something more about the woman standing before her.

Dinner proved not to be as enlightening as Alyson had hoped. The conversation turned to the role of the church today in God's plan and since Alyson knew very little about the topic, that left Kathy and herself to carry on little tidbits of conversation. She did take the time to observe Beth as the meal progressed. The way she sat tall in her seat. The way she held her fork as she ate and most especially the way her eyes lit up when she spoke about God. Even her voice was filled with a certain reverence and love, yes love. When she spoke of God it was as if she knew him almost intimately which didn't make any sense at all because after all God is a God and not a person in the flesh. Alyson admitted that she didn't know what to make of this. She could feel a tug on her arm.

"Are you happy you found your sister?" Kathy asked.

All conversation at the table stopped and Alyson looked at Kathy not knowing what to say. She could feel all eyes staring at her, waiting for her to say something. She could feel familiar eyes compelling her to confront them. She looked at Darrell and then in resignation faced familiar eyes and yet not. Eyes that seemed to probe her very being that left no corner of her mind untouched. In that instant she knew that this woman *knew* her. Not just her name and phone number. That was superficial stuff. This woman knew her deepest and innermost self. This woman was acquainted with her heart and soul!

She understood what she had not before for she had been trying to gain understanding through natural means and she was still at a loss. She needed to adjust her thinking and approach this woman on her own ground. Spiritual ground. Looking into the eyes, familiar eyes, she saw approval in their depths. It was as if she could read her very thoughts. Tearing her eyes and thoughts away from that which was unfathomable as well as unfamiliar, Alyson looked again at Kathy for there was safety in the eyes of a child.

"Kathy I know that Beth looks an awful lot like the picture you saw of my sister and when I saw her for the first time, I thought she was my sister too, but she's not my sister." She carefully explained to the little girl.

"OH!" Kathy said.

Chapter 8

Dinner was over shortly and though Darrell invited everyone back to his home, Beth declined. They left her at her apartment, but before the car drove off, she slipped Alyson a folded note.

They said very little on the drive to Darrell's house. Once there, Kathy changed then went in search of her friend who lived next door, leaving them alone.

"How about some tea?" Darrell asked.

"I'd like that. Is there anything I can do to help?" Alyson asked needing something, anything to do.

"No, it won't take but a minute."

In Darrell's absence, Alyson pulled the note that Beth had given her from its place in her purse. She unfolded it and slowly read it.

Alyson, I know that you had hoped to find your sister in me. Things are not always as they appear to be. I know that your faith has wavered these many years, but there is a passage of scripture that I would like you to read. I Corinthians Chapter 13 verses 9 through 13.

P.S. I know that you own a bible. I will see you tomorrow, same time at the mission.

By the time she had finished reading the note, Darrell was calling from the kitchen to tell her that the tea was ready. She had no idea what to make of Beth's note.

"There's still a lot of this beautiful evening left. Why don't we take our tea out to the patio?" He suggested as he held open the door leading to it.

Alyson found a delight to her senses as her eyes took in the beauty of her surroundings and she could smell the fragrance of the flowers that were in bloom. There was a path that led to a gazebo inviting one to just sit and read.

"Darrell it's absolutely beautiful. The landscaping is breathtaking! Did you do all this?"

"No, I'm afraid that I don't have a green thumb." He laughed as he held up both thumbs for her to see then directed her to join him on a floral padded glider that was just the right size for them both to sit comfortably. "The garden was Melissa's domain. After she passed, I hired a professional landscaping company to keep things going. It would have been such a shame to let it all die with her."

"Does it still hurt?" Alyson asked touching his arm, concern in her voice.

"No it doesn't hurt anymore. What Melissa and I shared was very special to me and I will always love her, but I know that she didn't want me to spend the rest of my life grieving for her."

"I can't imagine how a person could get through something so devastating to a spouse. I remember when Alicia left us. I was so angry and hurt. How did you make it through?" Alyson asked wanting very much to know.

"Melissa and I are strong Christians and when we first received the news about the cancer, we relied heavily on our faith that God would see us through and that our faith would be enough to heal her. Even when she grew progressively worse and the chemotherapy that was suppose to be helping seemed to have the opposite effect and even when we were told by the doctors to prepare for the inevitable, we held on to our faith. Even when she took her last breath, we held on to our faith."

"How could you even then?" Alyson spoke her voice barely above a whisper, her own lack of faith surfacing.

"After she passed, I was in utter and complete confusion. I couldn't understand why our faith hadn't been enough. My pastor, who is also my good friend, helped me get through that time and helped me to find understanding and peace."

"How?" Alyson asked the simple question.

"First he reminded me that no matter what happens God is still God. You see Alyson what we desire for us and what God desires for us are two very different things. We all have a set time on this earth. It was Melissa's time. We don't all get to live until we're old and gray. We don't get a choice in how we enter this world or how we leave it. But we do get a choice in how we live the time that is given to us. I have no regrets about my life with her. I didn't find real peace though until Gerald, my pastor and friend, helped me to remember a biblical truth that Melissa kept saying to me before she passed."

"What?" Alyson asked in wonder of the faith that this man beside her possessed.

"To be absent from the body is to be present with the Lord. The moment she closed her eyes on earth, she opened them in heaven. Though she was no longer here with us, she is where all saints look forward to being. She's in eternity with our Lord and Savior. Remembering that helped me to let her go."

This last statement prompted Alyson to remember how she had felt about her sister's disappearance. What if she were gone, gone in the way that Darrell's Melissa was. To this day she hadn't been able to let go. She mentally shook herself. No it wasn't the same, not the same at all. Alicia was here. She was back. Wasn't she?

Alyson remembered the note. "Darrell when Alicia, I mean Beth. I'm so confused! I don't know what I mean or what to call her! Anyway when we dropped her off at her place she handed me this note," she said placing the note in Darrell's hands.

"First Corinthians Chapter 13 verses 9 through 13," he read.

"I'm not sure why she gave this to me," Alyson said her brow knitted in confusion.

"Paraphrased I know the scripture, but I'll get my bible." He left but returned shortly caring a soft leather bound bible. He found the scripture and began to read.

119

9. *For we know in part, and we prophesy in part*

10. *But when that which is perfect is come, then that which is in part shall be done away.*

11. *When I was a child, I spake as a child, I understood as a child, I thought as a child: but then I became a man, I put away childish things.*

12. *For now we see through a glass darkly; but then face to face: now I know in part; but then shall I know even as I am known.*

13. *And now abide faith, hope, charity, these three; but the greatest of these is charity.*

"I'm still not sure what it means," Alyson said utterly confused.

"Well it means that what we know of God and His plan for life, is such a small part of the whole. When Christ comes again He is that which is perfect. Then all that we know or even think we know will be put to rest and we will finally understand the whole of it all." Darrell explained. "When we are first saved. That is, when we first accept that God is real and that He sent His only Son, Jesus Christ to save us from our sins, we come to God in a sense like babies. Our natural progression is growth, much like what an actual baby goes through to adulthood. We don't know a lot at first but we study and we seek God for understanding and enlightenment and He reveals Himself to us. We continue to learn and to grow as Christians through-out our journey here on this earth."

"I think I'm beginning to understand," Alyson said.

"In verse twelve, 'Now we see through a glass darkly,' glass serves as a barrier but allows you to see out, and it also serves as a reflector. In the glass we see ourselves as we really are." Darrell stopped for a moment.

Alyson watched as he grappled with finding the right words to convey to her what he intended to say.

"Have you ever tried to look out the window at night?"

"Yes it's hard to see even when I put my face really close to the glass," Alyson interjected.

"That's how it is with us as Christians now. It's hard to comprehend all that God is and all that He has planned for us even once we understand who we are *in* Him. But when we see Him face to face, in that day, it will all be clear. In the final verse, it talks about faith, hope and charity, which is love. And the greatest of these is love. You see Alyson, without love it is impossible to have faith or hope in anything or anyone. Through love stems forth that which gives life its very meaning."

Alyson thought about what Darrell had just said and realized that there was so much she didn't know or understand about what he and Beth and Alicia held so dear. They sat in silence for a moment. "Darrell tell me more," was all she could say.

Alyson wasn't sure how long they sat with Darrell sharing with her His God and His ways and His word and she listening intently asking questions with a desire to know the truth that she had never known was in her.

The evening shadows grew long as the sun began to set in the evening sky, so too did it set on her unbelief and her faithlessness and in their place sprang forth the beginning of understanding, faith, belief and love for a God that would love her even with all her imperfections.

"Darrell, I've been so long in denial of God. Where do I and how do I fix this?" Alyson asked in reference to the life she had been living without God and completely at a loss to explain her newly found faith and what to do with it.

"Do you believe that God is Lord and creator of everything?"

"Yes," Alyson said.

"Do you believe that Jesus Christ, the only begotten Son of the Father, died for your sins that you might have life here and through-out eternity?"

"Yes, I believe," she said in wonderment.

"Do you believe that Jesus is now risen and is seated at the right hand of the father?"

"Yes, I believe!"

"Then I want you to pray this prayer with me." He said as her took both her hands in his.

Lord God, forgive my sins. I acknowledge that You are God, the only true and living God. I accept Your gift of salvation for me through Jesus Christ Your only Son. In Jesus' name I pray. Amen.

"Darrell I feel free!"

Alyson decided to take the week off so that she could sort through things and decide on a course of action in regards to all that had happened.

In the days that followed she found her life slipping into a pattern that was not quite of her choosing and yet she didn't consciously try to steer things differently. She would go in search of Beth and usually found her at the mission. Much to her amazement she found herself helping out also. She, Alyson Edwards took on the role of caregiver, hands on not administrator. She made sure the pregnant women got prenatal care at a local clinic and made sure the babies and the children were immunized. She made beds and helped in the kitchen. It really felt good! Later she and Beth would either go out to eat or go back to Beth's where she would whip up something delectable for them. This caused her some concern for Alicia possessed the same such culinary talents. She had resolved not to press Beth for answers to questions she seemed unwilling or unable to answer.

Even though she still knew so little about Beth, she knew that Beth was happy about her induction into the family of God. They would talk for hours about God and His word. Alyson was in awe when Beth spoke of Him and she desired for herself that kind of relationship with Him. After returning home she would phone Darrell and they would talk and he would tell her more. They would even study the bible on the phone! And she loved it!

She still hadn't told her parents about Beth nor had she contacted the police. She wasn't quite ready. On the other hand she was taking Darrell and Kathy over to her parents for dinner on Friday night. Her mother was pressing her to meet the new man in her life who had brought her daughter to a light in which she herself had been unsuccessful.

It was Thursday evening and Alyson had just returned from a day with Beth. She could hear the phone ringing as soon as she opened the door to her apartment. She picked it up just before the answering machine would have done so.

"Hey girl, why haven't I heard from you?" The voice on the other end sternly admonished.

"Shelly! How are you?" Not waiting for an answer, "I e-mailed you days ago and never got a response." She laughed into the receiver.

"Okay, okay, I'm just now as we speak checking my e-mails and just as you say there is one from you!"

"So why haven't you answered my e-mail?" It was Alyson's turn to do the admonishing.

"Our division has been in crises all week and demanded all hands on deck. All work and no play. I'm just now getting a chance to get some personal time in."

"Problem solved?"

"Yes and not a moment too soon! I hate it when we go on lock down. One minute more and I would have strangled my fellow colleagues!" Shelly laughed. "Now what's been going on with you? How did your dinner date go?"

It seem like months had past since last Friday night. "The dinner was great, but you'll never guess what happened." Alyson didn't know where to begin so much had happened as a result of that dinner.

"What? You actually enjoyed his company. Are you going to see him again? Tell me everything, the bills on me!"

Alyson told her everything.

"Wow," was all Shelly could say when Alyson had finished bringing her up-to-date.

"Now I don't know what to do." Alyson said.

"Have you thought about DNA testing to see if she's really Alicia?"

"No not really. I've been too busy to think about exactly what I should do." Alyson said.

"They can do amazing things with that these days. A string of hair or anything from a person can show distinctly who they are. And what about fingerprints? No two people have the same fingerprints."

"But to do that I would have to go to the police and I'm not so sure that I want to do that at this time." Alyson said the uncertainty evident in her voice.

"Alyson I think it's the only way you're going to know for certain."

"I know." Alyson agreed with her friend. "Shelly it may sound strange, but I'm almost afraid to know for certain even though the not knowing has been hard all these months. I know I'll have to make a decision to do something soon."

"Well keep me posted. Okay?"

"I will and Shelly," Alyson waited until she heard Shelly's 'yes' in response, "Answer your e-mails!"

Chapter 9

Darrell and Kathy picked her up at her apartment on Friday evening at 6:30 pm.

"Are you sure you're up to meeting my parents?"

"Absolutely," Darrell said resolutely.

"I'm sure glad he finally decided on a shirt. Every few minutes he was asking me which one looked better!" Kathy said from the rear seat.

"Okay, okay, so I'm just a little nervous." He said grimacing at Kathy, then laughing.

"Well I'm warning you now, my mother is the talkative one, while my father is more of the silent type, but he's a great guy."

After the introductions, Alyson's mother ushered them into the dining room for dinner. Alyson watched as Darrell talked easily with her parents. They laughed and enjoyed one another's company. She wanted them to like him and his daughter. The realization that she wanted this sense of family and fellowship surprised her. After dinner her dad kept Darrell and Kathy busy in the family room while Alyson helped her mother clear the table.

"I like your young man Alyson," her mother said as she began putting the dishes into the dishwasher.

"Mom, he's not 'my young man' as you put it." Alyson said unable to hide the smile the words evoked.

"You like him don't you."

"Yes I do mom. He's a really nice guy and Kathy's a great little girl." Alyson was silent for a moment. "Mom how could I have lived all these years without knowing the truth? You, Dad and Alicia tried. Why now? What's so different about this time? I believe that God is and it has made me so happy and so complete. I've learned so much this week that it feels as if I've lived a whole lifetime in just a few days." Alyson watched her mother who had tears in her eyes, cross the distance that had separated them not just in the natural as now but spiritually and embraced her child who was now a child of God.

Honey, I'm so happy. I've prayed for this."

"I know Mom."

It was late when they arrived back at her apartment so Darrell and Kathy left after making sure she was safely inside with a promise that he would call her when he got home. Alyson got ready for bed and waited for his call. She answered the phone when it rang sometime later.

"Hi, we made it home okay."

"That's good. So what did you think about my parents?" Alyson said.

"I like them," he said simply.

"They like you too." Alyson said and she was pleased at how well the evening had gone. They talked only a short time before saying goodnight.

Saturday turned out to be another beautiful day! Alyson made breakfast and enjoyed the morning. She had been working on a plan to jar Beth's memory back to reality, but she knew conditions had to be perfect and until this very day, no such opportunity had presented itself. She had spoken to her mother and through the course of their conversation had found out that her parents would be out most of the day attending their church bazaar. It was nice of her mother to invite her also but she declined, her mind already cementing her plan. Beth wouldn't be working at the mission today and they had already planned to meet for lunch. Afterwards all Alyson had to do was take her to her parent's home. Surely being there surrounded by a lifetime of memories and the spirits of the people who know you and love you faults and all, totally unconditional, would jar her memory!

Her plan was unfolding as she knew it would right up until the part where she drove her car up to her parent's home and turned to Beth so that she could study her reaction. Alyson had envisioned that there would be the dawning of the return of Beth's memories of herself as Alicia, but there was no reaction at all. Alicia did not come forth. Undaunted, Alyson opened her door to get out.

"Should I get out also?" Beth asked.

"Yes. It shouldn't take long. I just need to pick up some things. Come on inside." Alyson said as she tried to mask her disappointment behind the smile she flashed Beth.

"This must be your parent's home." Beth said.

A small flame of hope kindled within Alyson. "How did you know?" She asked trying to sound nonchalant as they made their way up the walkway.

"Because the mailbox has the same name as your own."

The kindled flame of hope extinguished. "Yes it's my parent's home. Why don't I give you the grand tour? Alyson covertly watched Beth as they moved through the rooms of the house, but her disappointment escalated, for it appeared as if Beth was seeing the house for the first time. The pictures on the family room wall and on the mantle of the fireplace drew no more attention than that of a polite stranger.

On the pretense of needing something from the kitchen, Alyson left Beth in the family room so that she could gather her scattered and torn emotions. She heard a car drive up but she thought it was just someone turning around in the driveway. Moments later a key turned in the lock of the kitchen door and Alyson felt trapped and unprepared to deal with it's meaning.

"Oh Alyson, Dad and I saw your car in the driveway. I didn't know that you were planning to drop by today. We've been having a wonderful time at the bazaar but I forgot one of the pies I was donating to the bake sale."

Alyson stood totally speechless watching her mother wrap the pie and then put it into a carrying case. She recovered enough to say, "I wanted to pick up a photo album so that I could show the pictures to Kathy and..."

The events that happened next seemed to happen all at once.

Beth came into the kitchen from the living room, "Alyson I..."

Her father came in the kitchen behind her mother and Alyson stood in the middle as all eyes collided on a central focal point and all seemed suspended in time as reality tried frantically to redeem the time.

Alyson was the first to recover. "Mom, Dad this is..."

"Alicia," her mother said though the way she said the name was as if she was asking a question.

Alyson watched as her mother went over to Beth and looked at her more closely.

"Alicia." She said as she touched Beth's face and looked into her eyes.

Alyson couldn't move or speak as she watched the scene before her. Her mother just stood looking into Beth's eyes, her hands on either side of Beth's face, for what seemed like an eternity. Then all of a sudden she dropped her gaze and her hands and turned to Alyson.

"Mom, Dad this is Beth. I know that she looks a lot like Alicia but..."

"She's not Alicia." Her mother said as if she knew for certain.

"It's nice to meet you Mr. And Mrs. Edwards. I'm not here to cause you any confusion. If you'll excuse me, Alyson I'll wait for you in the car."

After Beth left the house, Alyson's dad came over to where mother and daughter stood. "Alyson if that's not Alicia, who is she?"

"Dad, Mom I met her at a mission last Saturday. She looks so much like Alicia but she claims that she isn't Alicia."

"Maybe she's suffering from amnesia." Her dad said sure that that must be the explanation.

"When I first met her I thought so too. She cooks like Alicia and she even sings like Alicia. She looks like Alicia, same body, same face, but..." She wasn't sure how to explain the rest.

But her mother finished what she wasn't able to. "Her eyes are the same and yet different and when I touched her, it was as if every fiber of my being was totally alive and my mind, my body and my spirit were in total agreement."

Alyson looked at her mother and knew too that that was exactly how she felt when she was with Beth and yet had not been able to put into the right words.

"Who is she?"

"I don't know Mom but I'm sure I'll find out soon."

Alyson pulled out of the driveway. Maybe it was time to go to the authorities. Maybe she should see if Beth would submit to DNA testing and allow herself to be fingerprinted. She wasn't ready to let go if there was any hope that she and her mother might be wrong. But didn't a mother know her own child? Alyson pushed the thought to the back of her mind.

"You still miss her. I can tell." Beth said.

"Yes I do."

"I'm not here to cause you more pain. I'm not here to cause you confusion."

"Why are you here?" Alyson asked as she pulled into a parking space in front of a group of small stores. She turned to Beth for an answer.

"I'm here to carry out my Father's plan."

"And what might that be, Beth?"

"It will all be clear in time for there is a season for all things."

Alyson reluctantly left it at that and she and Beth spent the afternoon perusing little antique stores. They decided to have dinner out and stopped at a small Chinese restaurant that Alyson loved. After they were seated and their order placed with the waiter, Alyson decided it was time to get a few answers.

"Beth you said to me that you know who you are and where you come from. If you're not Alicia, who are you and what do you mean by you know where you come from?" Alyson said as she searched Beth's face and waited for her to speak.

"Alyson we are all spirit beings. We were with God before He formed the world. God Himself is a spirit and when we have a relationship with Him and when we worship Him, we worship Him in spirit and in truth. The truth is His word. All of us, everyone in the world who excepts Him as God and believes in His Son Jesus as the Christ and Savior of the world, will all go back to God and live with Him in eternity."

Both women stopped as the waiter came back with the food they had ordered.

"You asked if I'm not Alicia then who am I. I am God's and He is mine. All that matters is the name that He has given me. All that matters is His plan and His purpose for me and the world."

"And what is His plan for you?" Alyson asked.

"To help those who are lost find their way to Him, to give those who are without hope the Hope of the world, to watch over His children, and to be guardian of His commandments," Beth said.

Alyson looked into Beth's familiar eyes and asked, "Is that what you truly believe?" She wasn't sure if she was looking at Beth or looking at Alicia.

"Everything for you in this world and the next hinges on what you know as truth. God is God whether one believes that or not. So everything for those of us, who belong to God, begins and ends with what you know as truth. I can't tell you how overjoyed I was when you told me of your own conversion to the truth! Do you know that the very angels in heaven rejoice every time one of His comes back to the fold?"

"Yes thanks to you first of all and to Darrell who has been patiently guiding me through the bible and teaching me about God. You both have helped me to understand what I was unwilling to know and unwilling to believe before."

"The important thing is that you believe and know now." Beth said as she patted Alyson's hand.

"You and Darrell have such a strong belief in your faith. It's all so new to me. Where and how do I begin to develop that kind of strength? There's so much I don't know."

"You've already begun." Beth said softly. "Your knowing the truth is the bases of your faith in God. Faith is that which causes one to believe to the point that one would put all their hopes and dreams and all they are into it even when there's no proof for the physical eyes to see. Here let me show you something." Alyson watched as Beth took a small bible from her purse.

"Chapter eleven of Hebrews in the New Testament is all about faith. When you get home tonight I want you to read it. In it you'll find the answers you seek and the strength you desire. In it you'll find that which you need to build on in order to go on. Promise me you'll read it tonight?"

Alyson looked into the face that was so intently awaiting her response. "I promise."

"Keep reading and studying the word of God and you'll be just fine. I know you probably have to get back to work next week. I can't tell you how much I've enjoyed spending time with you this week."

"I've enjoyed it as well." Alyson said. "I've done things that I never in a million years thought I would. But it feels great!"

"I can tell you enjoyed it!"

The two women laughed together.

"It feels like it's been a year instead of just one week, so much has changed in my life," Alyson said.

"The change is in you. You will find that life around you will go on as usual. It is up to you to begin the change in your world."

Alyson contemplated this for a moment and thought to herself, "It's one thing to change ones self, but how do you change a whole world?"

"You change the world one person at a time," Beth said.

Alyson looked at the woman across the table in astonishment for it was as if she had read her mind! Even if she claimed she wasn't Alicia it was nice having a sister again. There would be time enough to figure out the other stuff.

Chapter 10

Later when she dropped Beth at her place, as Beth was walking away, she turned back to look at Alyson and started to speak but seemed to change her mind. As Alyson drove away she looked in the rearview mirror and Beth was still standing as she had left her, looking after the retreating car.

How odd Alyson thought later as she prepared for bed. She knew that Beth had wanted to say something. She could see it in her eyes and yet she hadn't spoken. Well there would be time to talk tomorrow, Alyson thought as she remembered her earlier promise to Beth and opened her bible to the book of Hebrews.

After reading the entire chapter, Alyson thought back on all those extraordinary people and marveled at their extraordinary faith in God. Then she turned off her bedside light.

And she dreamed.

The trees were heavy with leaves. The ground beneath her feet was soft and covered with fallen leaves and wild flowers. She knew that she had come here before and yet it looked as if no one had ever come here for there was no worn path. Her feet moved of their own as if they knew the way. They took her to a waterfall that was in a clearing in the midst of the dense foliage. The water was falling softly. She couldn't see its beginning or its end. Looking around her she saw animals and even birds and yet something seemed not usual until she realized that that which seemed unusual was the lack of sound. All around her was life and yet there was no sound except that of the waterfall and it was so soft that even standing close to the water she had to strain to hear it. She sat on a large rock near the falling water, close enough that she could reach out and feel the water run over her extended hand. She cupped her hand and drank of it. It was cool and unlike any water she had ever tasted. As she drank her fill of it and looked around at this place that she had no prior knowledge of and yet knew that she had been here before, peace such as she had never known filled her. She looked into the water and saw in it her reflection and then a ripple came across the water and when the water stilled again there was a face on either side of her own. One Alicia and one Beth.

Alyson awoke with a start and sat upright in bed. The dream again! She had had this dream the day of Alicia's disappearance. She'd had it again on the day that marked one year of her disappearance. She had dreamt it again the day she met Beth and then now. She glanced at her clock amazed that it was almost nine o'clock in the morning!

There was only one person who could answer the questions she had and there was only one person who could tell her what the dream meant. She showered and dressed quickly, not sure why she felt this sense of urgency but she knew that she had to find Beth and find her soon.

Parking her car outside Beth's apartment, she literally ran to the door. She had been knocking for what seemed like an eternity and yet the door remained unopened and her repeated calls to it's occupant remained unanswered. Alyson barely noticed the door opening down the hall, but she did notice the cat that came to rub itself against her bare leg.

"She's not there. Are you Alyson Edwards?"

When she heard a voice say her name she turned immediately in the direction from whence it had come.

"I'm the landlady of this building." The owner of the voice said. "Are you Alyson Edwards?" She repeated the earlier question.

"Yes I am."

"She's not there." She said pointing to the door that had not responded to Alyson's repeated knocks. "She left about an hour ago. Strange thing though," the landlady said almost as if she where talking to herself, "she was paid up for the next six months, but when she stopped by to ask me to give you this, she said she would be leaving town and wouldn't be returning."

She handed Alyson an envelope that had a post-it note on the outside that said, "You know where to find me."

"Thank you," Alyson said and was down to her parked car before the landlady could respond. She knew! The car headed in the direction of the park. Ridge State Mountain Park. The unopened envelope lay on the passenger seat where she had tossed it.

The park was quiet this time of day. There were few cars in the parking lot. Alyson grabbed the envelope and ran through the trees to the small clearing. Somehow she just knew where to go. The *where* was the place where more than a year ago, they had found the last physical trace of Alicia. Her handkerchief.

Her eyes quickly scanned the small area and spotted Beth near the small waterfall with her back turned to her.

"Beth," she called out softly. "I knew you'd be here. Why? How did you know?"

"Alyson I want you to take a really good look around you," Beth said as she turned toward her.

Alyson did as she was asked and slowly realization dawned. *This* was the place in her dream! The day that she had come here with the police she had been too distraught to notice, and she had not come again until now. She looked in wonder for it was as if she had stepped into her own dream!

"You recognize this place don't you?" Beth spoke again.

"Yes." Alyson said in an expelled breath of wonder. "I was here the day that Alicia disappeared, and a year later on that same day. I was here the day that I found you. And last night I was here. What does it all mean?"

"Alyson, God speaks to us in many different ways. In this case He chose a dream, but He knew that you would need an interpreter to help you understand, so He sent me. That is why I am here."

"I don't understand," was all that Alyson could say for at that moment her eyes seemed fixed upon the sight before her. With the sun shining brightly through the clearing it appeared as if Beth herself reflected its brightness. As Beth began to speak her words seemed to infuse her very being, comforting her and dispelling her fears and doubts.

"I was sent by God to tell you that He knows that you loved her and that you love her still."

Alyson knew that Beth was speaking of Alicia.

"God wants you to know that He loves her too and that her life on this earth gave Him much joy. He was pleased with her service to human kind, her selflessness, her obedience and her sacrificial living. God has seen the pain that her absence has left. He has seen your confusion. He sent me to bring understanding and peace for He is not the author of confusion."

Alyson remained still, listening, unable to move, her eyes never wavering from Beth's own.

"You see Alyson, Alicia had achieved a level in her relationship with God that He desires of all His children, but few actually attain on earth. Alicia was one of the few. Her love was so pure and so profound that her praise was pure praise. A praise that touched the heart of the Father beyond measure." Beth paused for a moment before continuing. "Last evening I asked you to read a passage of His word. I said to you that it contained the answers you desired. Did you?"

"Yes." Still she couldn't say more.

"There was one in particular that possessed faith like that of Alicia's. His word says:

> *By faith Enoch was translated that he should not see death; and was not found, because God had translated him: for before his translation he had this testimony, that he pleased God.*
> *But without faith it is impossible to please Him: for he that cometh to God must believe that He is, and is a rewarder of them that diligently seek Him."*

Beth continued, "Alicia's work here was finished and so rather than see death, He took her and brought her directly into His presence, which was her earnest desire."

"Alicia's in heaven?" Alyson's voice seemed confined to that of a whisper.

"Yes."

The one word spoken softly by Beth, reverberated in her ears, ricocheting off her mind then her heart and found its resting place in her spirit and her very soul. She knew that what she was hearing was unquestionably the truth.

"Alicia had one other desire that had not come to pass before her time here was complete but God in his infinite wisdom had already predestined a time and a place. She desired that you, her beloved sister, be saved. The sister whom she shared life from the womb through earth's experience, be saved in order that it not end here, but that you would be able to share eternity with one another. The letter is from her. Read it and know that after God, she loved you most."

"But how?" Alyson asked.

"Nothing happens that God does not allow. The time has come for me to go. God will be with you and I assure you that we shall meet again, not in this earth, but in heaven."

It seemed as if the very sunlight grew brighter somehow, but Alyson couldn't look away and then Beth was gone.

Alyson stood fixed and unmoving as an overwhelming feeling surrounded her. It was as if it were an actual *presence*. Her mind searched diligently to put a name to it. *His Holy Presence*! And there was peace. Peace! Peace! Peace was all about her, in the trees, in the breeze and in the waterfall itself. Something that she had heard came to mind. Jesus said that whosoever drinks of the water that He gives shall never thirst. In her dream she remembered that even though there was life all around her only the water made a sound and she had drank freely of it. *Living Waters*!

She opened the envelope and read the letter penned in Alicia's unforgettable script:

Dear Alyson,

We've shared so much in this life. It has been my privilege to have shared this journey with you. I love you beyond measure. I thank God for His persistence in our salvation. I thank Him for loving us in spite of our shortcomings. I thank Him for calling us son's and daughters and joint heirs with Christ in His kingdom. He loves you sister.

The handkerchief was left for you to find. I no longer need it, for He has wiped all my tears away.

My work here is done, but yours is just beginning.

We will meet again.

I love you,

Alicia

Alyson didn't even realize that tears were streaming down her face. All the sadness of the past year was gone. It was gone! In its place she felt such joy, and such wonder. And such peace.

She could hear someone calling her name, a familiar voice. Then a soft gust of wind seemed to lift the note from her fingers taking it up high above the trees and as it reached the point where she had to shield her eyes from the noonday sun it looked as if the very paper itself grew wings and flew into the heavens. Alyson stood looking in awe and wonder. "Thank you God," she whispered to the sky.

She heard her name again, this time closer and she turned, reluctantly breaking the connection between earth and sky, with a Being so powerful and yet so gracious and loving that He would send on of His angels to save her and put her fears to rest! Her, Alyson Edwards! The thought was almost too awesome to comprehend!

Darrell came to stand beside her. She looked into his eyes and they answered her unspoken question. He had witnessed what she had seen. All he said though was, "What an awesome God!"

Alyson took his hand, "He sure is Darrell. He sure is!"

The End

Caught Up

A Note From The Author

If God Is and I know He is, the same yesterday, today and forever more, my imagination simply proposes: if He did it once, if He did it twice, might He not do it again?

Caught Up

About the Author

L.A. Fowlkes, named Lizzie by her parents, has been enthralled by written words for many years. Only in recent times has God given her the vision and the revelation to use those words for His purpose and the building of His kingdom.

She currently resides in Georgia with her husband and three children.

Caught Up

Order Form

Caught Up

by

L.A. Fowlkes

Give this wonderful book to your friends and colleagues.

Check your local bookstore or order here.

Please send _____ copies @ $9.99 each $_____

Shipping

$3 each book ($1 for each additional book) $_____

Georiga residents please add 6% tax $_____

Canadian/Mexico residents $5 each book $_____

Total $_____

Send order to:
FowlkesBooks
P.O. Box 862
Lithonia, GA   30058
770 982-8980
www.fowlkesbooks.com

Checks & Money Orders payable to: FowlkesBooks